Ross Watkins is an author and illustrator for both children and adults. His first major publication was as the illustrator of *The Boy Who Grew Into a Tree* (2012), and his picture book *One Photo* (2016) was shortlisted for the CBCA 2017 Picture Book of the Year. His short fiction has been published in various Australian anthologies and journals, and he was shortlisted for the 2011 Queensland Premier's Literary Award for Emerging Author. Ross lives on the Sunshine Coast hinterland. *The Apology* is his first novel.

T0307267

ROSS WATKINS **THE**
APOLOGY

UQP

First published 2018 by University of Queensland Press
PO Box 6042, St Lucia, Queensland 4067 Australia

www.uqp.com.au
uqp@uqp.uq.edu.au

Cover design by Christabella Designs
Author photograph by Claire Watkins
Typeset in 12/17 pt Bembo Std by Post Pre-press Group, Brisbane
Printed in Australia by McPherson's Printing Group, Melbourne

 This project is supported by the Queensland
Government through Arts Queensland.

  The University of Queensland Press is
assisted by the Australian Government
through the Australia Council, its arts
funding and advisory body.

ISBN 978 0 7022 6019 3 (pbk)
ISBN 978 0 7022 6151 0 (ePDF)
ISBN 978 0 7022 6152 7 (ePub)
ISBN 978 0 7022 6153 4 (Kindle)

 A catalogue record for this
book is available from the
National Library of Australia

University of Queensland Press uses papers that are natural, renewable and
recyclable products made from wood grown in sustainable forests. The logging
and manufacturing processes conform to the environmental regulations of the
country of origin.

For my mum and dad.
For my brothers.
For me.

He thinks of the letter only as The Apology. The object itself – the paper, its handwriting a juvenile scrawl – is gone, taken back by the writer. But its words have imprinted themselves on surfaces far more difficult to put in a pocket and walk away with: the membrane beneath his skull, the inner workings of his eyes. And his mouth. Always his mouth.

When he thinks of The Apology, he remembers the silkiness of cock skin sliding across his mouth.

The Apology was not asked for, nor was it expected. It was delivered in a way which told him that its author still possessed the ability to infiltrate and manipulate – now more than ever, even. To have somehow gained access to his house, leaving the letter on the bedside table, tucked between the pages of *The Stories of John Cheever* – that required resourcefulness, and guile. To know where to place the letter so that only he would discover it as he butterflied the book open. To know that he would find it in the moment he had sloughed off the muck of his day and allowed his body to rest, red wine on his breath, his mind groomed for the sluice of someone else's words.

He didn't read the letter. Not then, anyway. He allowed the writer his deviousness but not the satisfaction of his words hitting home. And so that night, when he didn't yet know the letter's contents, it only said one thing: *I am still touching you.*

ONE

ONE

ADRIAN

Mr Havlicek called this place his island. The assembly address was one of his favourites. It was over the top – everyone in the school knew that – but he delivered it whenever a sense of unrest was growing, or when a particularly appalling incident had happened among the student body. And there was a bit of both going on that day.

'The school,' he said, 'must be a safe place amid the troubled waters of the Western Sydney community. Here, within these grounds, we must set a high standard of morality. If we don't' – and here he paused, looking around the hall and its standing rows of bored boys in blazers – 'if we don't, then depravity will find a method to blot this school and everything that is good in it. You are boys becoming men, and in that becoming you must shed the puerile ways of boys.'

Boys, Adrian thought. *If they're not trying to fuck with you, they're trying to fuck with you.*

Mr H – everyone called him Mr H – dismissed the assembly to the sound of bags being slung over shoulders and murmured relief. He placed the microphone on its stand and descended the stage stairs to the hardwood floor. He walked directly towards Adrian, but did not look at him. 'Mr Pomeroy,' he said as he neared.

'Yes, Mr Havlicek?'

'My office.'

'Yes, Mr Havlicek.'

★

Adrian didn't know where to put his hands – pockets, knees. Across his chest. He knew why he'd been called in – a parent had complained that he'd been excessively late in handing back the Year Eleven English papers, a comparative analysis of *The Hunger Games* and Richard Connell's *The Most Dangerous Game*. The accusation was accurate – he had grown careless of his professionalism over the past term. He'd been teaching at the boys' high school for seven years, and already he felt the onset of burnout. The students seemed to like him, and their parents only complained about small things every so often, but in a place like that nothing could be taken for granted.

Mr H closed the door, then walked around his desk and sat in his chair. His breath was audible. He leant against the backrest, glanced at his desk, rubbed his moustache, and then looked at Adrian. 'Alex Bowman,' he finally said.

Adrian was very familiar. 'Akker' was what Alex liked to be called now, especially around the boys in class. He waited for Mr H to continue.

'Alex came to see me before assembly today, and he was quite upset. He was in that very chair and in tears. Distraught is probably a more apposite word, in fact.'

Adrian tried to imagine Akker in tears.

Mr H fiddled with his tie. A check tie on a check shirt. 'You see, Alex was here to make certain allegations, Mr Pomeroy. Allegations of a very serious nature.'

'I'm sorry?'

Mr H's moustache didn't move. 'I would be very careful with my apologies, Mr Pomeroy, if I were you. Especially at this point in proceedings. For reasons I can and cannot understand, Alex has not mentioned these allegations to his parents. He apparently felt more comfortable telling me in the first instance, and requested that I be present when he does tell them, so I have arranged a meeting with them and the school counsellor here at four-thirty today. This will provide you with sufficient time to gather your personal items and leave the school grounds. It is safer that way.'

Later, Adrian would try to imagine his own expression at hearing this. He did not have the presence of mind to gauge himself in the moment. He only felt heat. An overriding sense of heat. He knew why.

'You must understand that there are protocols for allegations of this nature, Mr Pomeroy,' Mr H said, but already Adrian was there and not there, dislocating, his eyes drifting to the school crest above Mr H's head – an open book below a hovering dagger, and the motto *Scientia Vos Liberabit*: Knowledge Shall Set You Free. Mr H went on about other details: that the police would be notified following the meeting, that failure to report the information was a criminal offence, that Alex's remarks were only allegations pending a full and proper investigation, and that the school must be seen to support the student, as it had a duty of care. That Adrian would be suspended with pay until further notice.

Mr H rubbed his moustache again. He moved small stacks of paper around his desk, then picked up a rogue pen and inserted it into his stationery caddy. 'If it appears that I am being careful with my words, Adrian, it's because I am.' He could no longer maintain eye contact.

Adrian again looked at Mr H. He understood the nature of the circumstances. 'Thank you,' he said, then he stood, pushed the chair to the desk and said, 'I am sorry.'

Adrian left the building.

★

Some boys were softer. They sat between the boy who believed he was above the learning process and the boy who was always talking about how good he was at overtly masculine things. Soft boys were easy targets, but sometimes they had an inner stability, a quiet confidence that could bamboozle the bullies and bullshit artists. And so, as Adrian had seen over the years, they got left alone. They became expert at evading conflict by smelling it before it ripened. They knew the right words to say at the right moment because they had become adept at strategising. It was their means of protecting their tender bodies from harm.

When Alex was twelve, back in his first year of high school, he was soft. A genuinely good kid, empathetic, and one with an academic future. Staff said he was the Year Seven standout, not because of his blond hair but as one of the school's low-socioeconomic successes, a poster boy for the school's scholarship program. Adrian had agreed. In English, the boy once wrote a short story which was a cut above the rest. Although his writing had its share of issues – spelling and grammatical errors and the like – the story was strong. It told of a boy not only well read but of remarkable sensitivity. Especially compared to the tales of violence and overstated heroism the rest always came up with.

Alex's story was about two feuding brothers in the afterlife, one on the verge of entering Hell and the other entering the gates of Heaven. The two men talk in armistice before saying goodbye. The unworthy brother talks about his regrets in life, and the worthy man listens. Despite their differences, the worthy man forgives his brother for his sins and announces that he may take his place in Heaven. The unworthy man declares that, although he desperately fears the flames, he cannot accept his brother's offer: he alone must bear the burden of his actions. He turns and enters the fire. Witnessing this, the worthy man feels great sadness and decides to go in after him, sacrificing himself so that his brother might have company. As the worthy man places a foot on the embers spilling from Hell, he hears a familiar voice calling from behind. He turns and steps towards the voice, only to find himself being carried by light through the gates of Heaven. On the other side of the gates, he finds that the voice belongs to his brother, who waits for him with open arms.

Adrian photocopied the story and showed it to some other teachers. He talked about it a lot for a few days, and it stayed with him over the next weeks. It became an anecdote he mentioned in class for the next three years.

Even back then, Adrian wondered if his compassion for Alex brought him too close to the boy. Did he see something of himself in his student? He asked himself this after writing Alex's Year Seven English report, when he realised he had stepped away from the usual objective expressions: Mikael is still learning how to negotiate the challenges of social interaction in the classroom, Jamal has tried his best to convey his ideas about the texts studied this semester, and so on. Instead, Adrian found himself being more heartfelt: Alex made being a teacher worthwhile, he wrote, and he loved having him in his class. That Alex was one of the loveliest boys Adrian had ever taught, and his talent for storytelling should be encouraged. He even wrote that he looked forward to being part of Alex's nurturing, in whatever way possible, during his high school years.

When Adrian read back over the report he was both proud and hesitant – the sentiment was genuine but its lack of distance made him wonder if he'd breached a boundary of some sort. He then thought about his mother, and the kindness of her tongue during his own formative years, and he left the report as it was. No ill came of it.

Four years later, when Alex again entered Adrian's classroom at the beginning of term, his mates called him Akker. Alex was still present in Akker's eyes but his face had firmed. Adrian had seen this metamorphosis before, of course, a thousand times throughout his time at the school, but he remembered none as pronounced as Alex's. The twelve-year-old body had stretched and strained itself well into pubescence; his mouth was more resolute, and his jawline testing stubble. He was still handsome, Adrian thought, but a more aloof and merciless kind of handsome.

After that first lesson, Alex made sure he was the last to leave. He approached Adrian's desk.

'What's up, Alex?'

'I'd like to be called Akker in class, sir.'

'Sure, Akker. Not a problem.' Adrian was grateful for the contact – the boy hadn't said a word all lesson. He'd just leant back in his chair with an expression which could have been derision, or boredom, or self-satisfaction. 'It's good to have you in my classroom again.'

Akker slipped his hands into his pockets and put on a smirk. 'I look forward to being nurtured, sir,' he said.

It was then that Adrian first felt the haunting heat of the past.

★

The heat came upon him again as he drove the M4 home. He rolled down his window and tried to settle his mind, his heartbeat. The truck tailgating him didn't help, its grille just about filling the rear windscreen. The word *cunt* came off his lips in a fluent way, and he wondered who it was truly meant for: the delivery driver, Akker or himself?

Akker …

The name echoed and he felt a pulse of angst. Soon the boy and his parents would be walking into Mr H's office, and that moustache would be announcing Adrian's professional demise and personal humiliation. Fuck.

Akker …

Adrian wondered about the story he'd tell this time – the words he would choose, the imagery, the villain writ large in the imagination of his audience.

Earlier, on his way to the English staffroom, Adrian had glimpsed himself in the reflective glass of the administration building. Although the horror of the afternoon wasn't yet there in the detail of his face, he still wondered what others saw in this thirty-six-year-old. His receding hairline and his beak-like nose were disconcerting self-criticisms, but soon the students would be saying more creative things about him – words passed between desks and published on Facebook and Twitter and wherever the fuck else. Years ago he'd done some casual teaching at state schools, and he preferred their kind of arsehole.

Those boys told you what they thought of you to your face, then maybe threw a rock at your car. But the boys at this school were in it for the game, and what depraved games they liked to play.

He tried the radio for a distraction and hit the four o'clock news. His father always said that the news was just other people's problems, and right now it was a good reminder that many people out there had it worse than him. There was an extended piece on the ISIS attacks in France, then something political. The next item was on the royal commission's investigations of child sexual abuse at a grammar school. Adrian turned it off.

He checked his rear-vision mirror: the truck was still behind, bearing down on him.

'Go around, fuckface!'

On his back seat was a box full of student papers, and Adrian realised how stupid he was to bring it all home with him. When he packed his stuff he hadn't been thinking, but now he recognised that this wouldn't be a short term layoff. It would be Akker's word against his – if he could find his words and not incriminate himself, that is. What would he tell people? He imagined himself arriving home and not coming out until the whole business was over.

Again, the heat. Blooming from his neck. He felt like ripping his shirt open.

He looked at his phone in the centre console and thought of Nguyet. He was coming home earlier than usual, but this wasn't unprecedented so he hoped for fewer questions. He would much prefer to tell her over red wine than over the doormat. He then thought of Tam. *God, young Tam* ... He pictured the boy's face, a pretty composite of Vietnamese and Caucasian features. At six he was asking so many questions but could not yet understand everything going on. How would the boy's impression of his father change with the knowledge of today?

Six years old … Now Adrian's own scars were being thumbed.

The intensity of the heat rose. He suddenly felt tightness across his chest and he breathed harder, quicker, but he was beyond settling himself now. The windscreen blurred as he thought of Tam's face, Akker's face, his brother's face, and it was then that Adrian lost consciousness. His head fell forward, his nose cracked against the centre of the steering wheel and the car veered left. The truck had backed off by now but the distance between the two vehicles wasn't enough to prevent it from bashing into Adrian's car, spearing it off the motorway and onto the grass, across a ditch and into a tree.

The truck kept motoring.

NOEL

Noel leant back on the bonnet of his car and felt far from everything familiar. No family, no cops, no more fucking grubs. The only familiarities were what he dragged out here with him and what he created – and the thing he created here was superb.

He sat with his knees bent and drank from a longneck of beer he'd bought from a drive-through in an outer suburb of Perth. Just some typical bottle-o in a bland suburb no one would think twice about, especially not in relation to a fire in scrubland east of the airport. If he did the right thing – if he stuck to his protocol – then the two actions were unrelated and the bottle shop's CCTV footage would mean zip. And out here at Statham's Quarry, where blokes came on Friday nights to drink and do doughies, there were no cameras, and Noel wasn't stupid enough to film the fire with his phone. Not like the dipshits who got pinched doing this stuff because they'd uploaded it and bragged online. Noel was above them and their narcissism – his was a compulsion he could control. In fact, that sense of control was what sparked his gratification.

From the car, he watched the smoke whirl white and brown,

which he guessed had something to do with the grass being consumed. It smelled sweet, and from two hundred metres away the crackle sounded like erratic applause, as if the land was celebrating his choice to burn it all back. Drinking the beer, he thought: *If only more than grass could be burned back.*

Noel wasn't a bad guy. Unlike other men he'd worked with, he hardly ever drank hard and never screwed any of the victimised women he came across in the job – the women begging for a hero, which was really anyone who didn't beat them. Nor was he like the two general duties officers he knew who spent their work hours fucking in the police vehicle. *Noel*, he told himself, *you're an officer for the Western Australia Police Force, and you're one of the good guys.*

He knew that if he was smart in his actions – if he applied enough thought before, during and after the event – then his chances of being caught were low. The statistics said that arson was one of the least convicted crimes because the evidence was usually burned. He doubted that a forensics team would be sent to a grassfire out in the middle of nowhere, but even if they were – if somehow something went wrong and the fire got out of hand – he had strategies to contain any evidence and prevent discovery.

He never went to the same location twice, although he had hit the Zig Zag a few times, plus Helena Valley. He always mapped out where he would park the car and which route to take out of there, and while he couldn't help tyre tracks, his tread was common enough. He always walked to the ignition location with bare feet, and only hung around long enough to see the flames take hold and feel the heat across his face. He watched the rest from back at the car.

He didn't use accelerants either. Accelerants could be traced, and they got on your hands and clothes. He didn't want Wendy asking why his pants smelled of petrol when she did the washing. But he did use an incendiary device. He came up with the idea for it during a drive out to a spot he'd had his eye on for a while, after some failed attempts to get a good one going elsewhere. Now he followed the same process each time. First he'd collect dried grass and leaves from the area and heap the materials in the middle of a sheet of folded newspaper. He then placed a box of matches on top, and folded the newspaper to make a neat package. The last step was to fix a cigarette to the package with a rubber band. It was simple and crude but the heat it generated almost always burned the box of matches completely, and liquidised the rubber band. He had tested it several times. The device was small enough to fit in his pocket as he walked into the scrub. When he found a good location he would light a cigarette, place it and leave it.

He also liked the feel of the device in his pocket. It had a density, and attached to this was a sense of reliability, of purpose. In his line of work, many actions made little sense, and it was his job to expose cause and effect – that's what a detective is supposed to detect. Sometimes he thought about his own relationships as a system of cause and effect; life seemed simpler that way, more manageable. Especially with Wendy. He knew that certain conversations were fire-starters in themselves, so he turned his back on those things more and more and chose to be quiet. There were still times when he just couldn't help himself, when holding back from saying something was harder than spitting it out – sometimes you just had to deal with the effects. He saw this as selective enforcement.

Noel drank from his beer and opened the scanner app on his phone to listen for the call over the radio. There was no need for the fire crews to use sirens out here so he had to take care. If he saw them coming, he knew it would be over for him – and he wasn't about to hang around and watch those guys do their business. He wasn't thrillseeking. This wasn't about endorphins.

He knew what he was doing was a criminal act, but it was minor compared to the brutality he encountered most days. When he thought about his intent, he found it impossible to gain a critical view of himself – offender profiling was part of his job, but the job also taught him that concepts like intent and motive were better left on the television screen. And he hated 'primetime crime', where the plot had to be kept so tight that real-life complexities were relinquished. People always wanted things to be neat and explainable because it assuaged their fears, but arresting the grubs out there showed him that if crime wasn't based on a complicated personal history, then it was all pretty much random acts of chaos.

Still, he could nail down the first time fire truly impressed him. A few years back he was investigating a case involving aggravated burglary and motor vehicle theft, where the car was found alight in the underground car park of a four-storey apartment building. The fire forced the evacuation of the residents, which was when he arrived on scene to see the fire eating up the last of the car's interior and paintwork and the plastics in the engine bay. The red and yellow of it was brilliant. Such a perfect intensity. Until that moment he'd thought of fire as an angry thing, but it wasn't like that at all. It was composed. Systematic. Not that he told anyone, but he felt satisfaction in watching it work. He had held back the fire guys as long as he could, but soon they got in there and snuffed it.

The blackened shell left behind was, by comparison, dreadful. He attached a different emotion to this image – something closer to disgrace. This was an emotion he knew well from older days, but carried with him now, like a phantom limb. It was always the undetectable that came to mean the most.

Noel spat into the mouth of his empty beer bottle and was wrapping it in the paper bag when he heard the call come in on the app. Good timing. He got into the car and put the bottle in the passenger footwell. From there it would make its way into a public bin on the way back home, twenty kays away as the crow flew. Easy as.

*

Dianella was a tidy suburb, what with all the Greeks and Jews, and Noel liked his house. It was a good house for a copper's family because it had a high fence built of rendered brick and the building sat a bit low from the road. Wendy hated it. She said it looked more like a police station than a home. She preferred the neighbour's place – a weatherboard joint with a row of lavender and a tree swing on the verge. She liked that kind of quaint shit.

When he got in Wendy was making dinner. She said hello, he said hey, and even from that brief contact he knew she was mentally elsewhere. When Wendy got distracted she became more methodical in her actions.

'You're a bit late,' she said.

He made a point by not taking his shoes off. Instead he walked past the kitchen bench, opened the sliding door to the patio and took a cigarette from its packet.

'Where are the girls?' he asked.

'Grace is in her bedroom, Riley's got guitar lessons.' She was slicing mushrooms – precisely. 'Where've you been?'

'Had a few beers with the boys.' He lit the ciggie, pulled deep.

'Oh,' she said. 'Simmo there?'

Simmo had been best man at their wedding, but on the piss he had also proved to be the worst man. Groping Wendy through her bridal dress was one notable act in a series Noel hadn't kept tally of. And while he had pulled Simmo up for being a wanker, the truth was that Noel didn't mind too much. Another bloke giving his wife attention made him feel kind of proud. Not that Wendy felt the same way.

'Yeah,' he lied. 'Behaved himself, though.'

'Glenda called earlier, and it's not your father this time.'

He made a sound which was meant to be nonchalance. He'd moved to the west coast to get away from his family, but the phone was a fucker which undid all that. At least his mum didn't have his mobile number.

'You'd better call her,' Wendy said.

He looked at the picture of mouth and throat cancer on his ciggie packet. It was bloody horrible but he'd somehow got used to it. So much so that he didn't feel he was really having a smoke now if he wasn't looking at some gory health warning.

Wendy came over to the door with a tea towel. She wiped her hands, then took her mobile from the sideboard. 'You'd better call her.'

He took the phone.

'It's Adrian.'

ADRIAN

Adrian regained consciousness inside the wreck. It was a vague sense of consciousness – he knew there were people outside the vehicle and his face was wet and his door was opened by a paramedic. The paramedic asked questions and Adrian believed he made answers with his mouth, though he couldn't be sure. There was pain in the centre of his face and pain across his chest. He wondered if he'd had a heart attack.

There was pressure around his neck, and now he was on a stretcher. He couldn't move his head. Soon there was movement and he felt that the car was getting further away. Then he was inside the ambulance. He felt a cannula go in under his skin, and it didn't take long before the sound was turned down. Adrian closed his eyes and went with the rhythm. There may have been a siren. He assumed there were lights. Next there came a gentle tapping. Maybe it was a check of his vital signs, or an oxygen mask, or something else entirely. But one thought repeated: *one tap means teeth, two taps means someone's coming.*

★

Adrian woke in a hospital bed. His vision was partially obstructed by a white object on his nose, and when he put his fingers to the whiteness he realised it was a dressing. He could tell that his left eye was swollen and there was a band of tape running across the dressing and onto his cheeks. There must have been a laceration, he realised, because if he closed one eye and used the other to look down at the bridge of his nose he could see a patch of blood.

His nose. The nose his grandfather on his mother's side gave him, and he'd gone and broken it. He'd never liked its shape but now it would spite him even more. And he'd have to put up with the dressing in the centre of his face, branding him as a victim. How ridiculous. It made him think of Jack Nicholson in *Chinatown*, spending most of the movie with a bandage over his nose after Roman Polanski slit his left nostril with a flick-knife. Adrian had always thought that having the hero going about his business with such a thing on his face was pure genius; yet Jack had been a nosy feller, and Adrian wondered if his own punishment was something similar – as if his involvement with Akker had invited a dark variety of cosmic justice. Despite the accident, he hadn't forgotten what Mr H told him.

He could move his head now, and as he tried to sit up there was still an ache in his chest, though the morphine nullified any acute pain. God bless analgesics. The bed curtain was closed but through the window he could see the rooftops of hospital buildings and cloud the colour of Sydney grey. It was getting dark, and for a moment he thought it a respite to be here in this bed with a view of the falling evening. Especially considering the alternative.

He could hear someone crying on the other side of the curtain and thought it might be Nguyet, so he said, 'Are you there, Noo?' but there was no response. He pressed the buzzer for the nurse.

The nurse came in and pulled the curtain back. 'Hi, Adrian,' she said. 'You're in Westmead Hospital. How are you feeling?'

Through a gap in the curtain opposite he saw a pale guy, perhaps in his late twenties, sobbing. It was a quiet sob – the midst of grief. His sheets were pulled up and so Adrian couldn't be sure, but he thought the guy might have lost both legs. The sheet flattened to the bed at his knees.

'Fine,' Adrian said. 'Fine enough, I suppose.'

'Can you tell me why you're here today?'

He looked at the nurse. He explained that he remembered certain aspects of the accident, like the sensation before blacking out, and she nodded. She didn't seem big on small talk. She told him what he already assumed about his nose, and then said that the chest pain was from the pull of the seat belt upon impact. Most people break their ribs, she remarked, so to suffer only deep tissue bruising was fortunate.

Good fortune was not the term Adrian would use to describe his situation. Good fortune was finding out that the four-thirty meeting hadn't gone ahead, or that Akker's parents hadn't believed his story, or that Mr H had dealt with the issue in another way, a less official way. Better still, good fortune was Akker telling Adrian's side of their truth ...

The nurse showed him the meal order sheet and he thanked her. Then, instead of asking about his wife – which he knew he should have done – Adrian said, 'Have the police come for me?'

★

When Nguyet and Tam arrived the food service lady was there with her trolley full of trays. Even though Adrian was a late admission and hadn't ordered his meal in time, she gave him a tray that was an extra. 'A man checked out,' she said.

Adrian wondered what she meant; in a hospital, he mused, there was checking out and then there was checking out. He wanted to point out the ambiguity, but thought better. He wasn't in the classroom. The correct word was *discharge* but that wasn't really much better.

Nguyet was visibly relieved to find Adrian awake and okay. She smiled at the service lady and closed the curtain once the trolley was wheeled away; although she'd been in Australia for seven years, she still found any public display of affection uncomfortable. She kissed Adrian's forehead and gently touched the swelling around his eye. She made cooing sounds.

Tam was sheepish, like he didn't know what emotion he was meant to feel. He was that kind of boy. Adrian remembered well the day the cat died, when Tam was only four. While Adrian dug a space in the herb garden, Tam had watched with an interested smile. 'This isn't the time for smiling, mate,' Adrian had said. Tam also smiled when his mother wrapped the cat in a blanket and placed it in the hole, and when Adrian smoothed the dirt over it and put some rocks on top. Tam looked at their faces, trying to understand the ceremony of grief. It was his first experience of death, and because he had never developed a meaningful attachment to the cat his only option was to act out sorrow, mirroring that of his parents. It was then that he had stopped smiling. When he did, Adrian regretted saying anything and wanted the boy to be himself. He had imposed his own emotions on his son.

Nguyet pulled a chair to the side of the bed, sat down and took Adrian's hand, kissing it. She asked how it all happened and he told her about the truck. She kept shaking her head.

'It's not that bad,' he said. 'I'm sure I've come out better than the car.'

She laughed a laugh of heartache.

Tam had climbed to sit on the edge of the bed. He stared at his father's face like he wanted to touch it. He then looked at the food tray, opened the lid on the meal and screwed up his mouth at the potato and beef. There was also a bread roll and a packet of butter. He picked up the roll. 'Can I have this?'

Adrian nodded. 'Sure.' He had no hunger, and anyway his face hurt.

Tam tore the roll open.

Nguyet put her head down on Adrian's arm, and he realised she'd never seen him so vulnerable. He touched her chin and bottom lip with his thumb, hoping that her affection would continue in the days to come. He was on the edge of a far greater vulnerability than a hospital bed. 'I guess you called Mum?' he asked.

She hadn't. Nguyet got along with Glenda, but Mal was another story. She'd held off calling.

'I'll do it when I get home,' he said. 'The less fuss, the better.'

Tam finished the roll and was now jamming a finger into the butter packet and licking it.

'You can eat the custard too,' Adrian said, and passed him the tub and spoon.

This is a good moment, Adrian realised, and he tried to hold on to the feeling because anxiety was building in him again. He had an intuition that the police were going to arrive soon, and a conversation would ensue involving enquiries about a matter of which his wife knew nothing – and which he didn't want to talk about right now. It would be an uneven encounter, too.

The police knew what Akker had said but Adrian didn't, and it was from this position of advantage that they would direct their questions.

He could phone Noel for advice but his brother would tell Glenda, and he didn't want her finding out that way. He didn't know how or when he'd tell her, but he wanted to retain that control. Plus, Noel was Noel. Since Adrian's wedding eight years earlier, the brothers only spoke once a year, if that. The last time was a random phone call about six months ago, with the stilted tone and awkward gaps of two strangers. No. Noel had gone to Perth for a reason, and the last thing he wanted was to be dragged back to the east coast by something like this.

Adrian had the thought that he was still inside a wreck.

★

When the police arrived, Tam was asleep on the end of the bed and the television was on with the volume low. A doctor came in with the officers and they introduced themselves.

But this wasn't yet the moment Adrian feared. The police asked questions about the accident, and he told them about the truck and blacking out. The doctor asked if Adrian had been experiencing a heightened level of personal stress; Adrian said that, no doubt, he had some unresolved issues at work. According to the police there was a case against the truck driver for negligent driving occasioning grievous bodily harm, but Adrian didn't want to pursue it. He suspected there'd be enough police attention soon enough.

The officers took his statement and informed him that he would be on a temporary conditional driving licence because he'd blacked out at the wheel. The doctor would refer Adrian to a psychiatrist; if the source of the stress was an ongoing issue, he was told, medication was available that might help reduce his anxiety.

And that was all. Adrian thanked them for their time.

Nguyet left soon after, with Tam asleep in her arms. She kissed him again and said she'd be back in the morning; she'd got her shift at the grocery store covered. She said she'd wait it out with him while the nurses did their observations to make sure he was fit to go home.

When he judged they were far enough away, Adrian finally let go. He cried hard but without sound. He cried on and off for over an hour, and when the crying was exhausted he called in the nurse to replace the dressing on his nose, which was soaked through. She said nothing as she crafted a fresh bandage out of wadding and tape. He appreciated the empathy he felt in her fingers, in their gentle application of pressure, and in her expression, even though she gave little away. He closed his eyes, and soon she was gone.

When he opened them again it was morning, and the amputee was sitting in a wheelchair, staring out Adrian's window.

*

Adrian was eleven when he saw Mal shut the door of the granny flat, which adjoined the rear of the detached garage. The flat was just one large room, with no kitchen but with a toilet in a small side room. The walls – both inside and out – were fibrocement, and there were a couple of holes where you could see through to the timber trusses. The lino was stained and had a faint animal smell, like dog piss; Adrian was convinced that a dog had had a litter in there.

When Adrian was eleven Noel was seventeen, and that year he'd claimed the room out the back as his own. He dragged in some old lounges from a council clean-up and had his mates over. Someone brought around an old television and hooked up a video player so they could watch American frat house movies. They put up posters of AC/DC and Cold Chisel, and on Friday nights they drank beer from cans as they sang 'Flame Trees' over and over.

'What goes on out there stays out there,' Glenda said firmly.

Mal said no smoking; although he himself went through a carton of ciggies a week, Noel was still a child and still under his roof, and the parents of kids who smoked were useless. Mal was a walking contradiction on some topics, and could be strikingly old-fashioned. One of Noel's mates was already eighteen and had a tattoo of Bon Scott on his forearm. When Noel came home with a tattoo magazine, Mal said that if the magazine was brought into the house he'd chuck Noel's stuff onto the kerbside and change the locks. Noel took the magazine to the flat out the back.

There was no lock on the door, and it was always left open anyway, unless there was heavy rain and someone thought to shut it, but Adrian hardly ever went in there. The only word he could think of to describe it was *seedy*, but there was more to it than just low light, pizza boxes and sticky lino. If that room showed what he had to look forward to when he grew into a young man himself, then he wanted to stay a boy forever. Yet even this idea of his youth was eventually obliterated. He was there when Noel and his mates thought it would be funny to show their dicks to each other and manipulate them like puppets, and he happened to be looking the day Mal went into the room.

Glenda was doing the groceries and Noel was somewhere else. Adrian was playing in his bedroom and through the window saw movement outside: his dad went into the granny flat and shut the door. Adrian kept playing with his superhero figurines, but he also kept watching the door, and kept wondering. Maybe twenty minutes later, Mal opened the door and went back into the garage to work on his car. It was then that Adrian decided to have a look around in there someday as well.

He walked home from school a bit quicker than usual one day that week and went in with his school bag and shut the door. He turned on the light and started looking behind the lounges and shifting cushions. There was a drawer under the TV with some videos, but that was all. There was the stereo, some tapes, a football on the floor. He picked it up and sat on the lounge. He then looked at the posters, which he knew covered the holes in the fibrocement boards. He leant over to one of the posters and pulled a bottom corner from the wall. He peered inside the hole and could see paper wedged there, so he reached in and felt for it. He thought it would be the tattoo magazine – perhaps his dad had been looking to get rid of it. But it wasn't what he expected.

And yet it was.

All that skin … The pictures of the women were confronting enough, but it was the men with their hairless bodies and hard cocks which stirred a dream he must have had almost half his lifetime ago. A dream he could only remember with vague tactility and as a murmur of sounds. He tried to remember more but couldn't. He only felt the onset of heat, as if all the blood in his body had rushed to his head. He'd uncovered something other than a porn mag, but he didn't know what.

Adrian put the magazine back and smoothed the poster corner down again. He picked up his bag, switched off the light and opened the door, and as he walked away he told himself that remembering the dream was the only important thing now. Regardless of how it made him feel, he needed to know what it meant.

At the time he didn't mention these things to anyone because he couldn't articulate his thoughts; that did not come until later, when he was fourteen or so and Noel had shifted to the Goulburn Police Academy. By then the granny flat had become a storage space for boxes of Adrian's old toys, Mal's engine parts and the stuff Glenda didn't really need but couldn't face throwing away. Noel's musty lounges and everything else, including the magazine, had gone – as had Adrian's grip on the dream he only might have had.

*

When Nguyet pulled into the driveway, she failed to notice the man in the car parked over the road. Adrian noticed.

Alex Bowman's father – Adrian couldn't recall his name right then – sat in a charcoal-grey Camry with the window down. For a moment Adrian wondered if he was there to beat the shit out of him, but the man didn't budge when they got out of the car and walked to the front door. While Nguyet was finding the house key, Adrian couldn't help looking across the yard and the road. Bowman looked back. As Nguyet pushed the key into the lock, Bowman mouthed some words Adrian couldn't decipher, and then put his head out the window and spat onto the bitumen. A car passed. Adrian went inside.

He spent the next hour in the lounge room watching

afternoon TV, trying to ignore the roil of his gut. His senses were amplified but at the same time he lacked mental clarity, as though emotion had exhausted his capacity to think. The television was meant to be a distraction, but he was distracted even from it, glancing through the blind every so often to check if the Camry was still there. It was, but he couldn't see Bowman because he had the window up now, and it was tinted enough to obscure what was within.

Adrian was sure he was there to intimidate, but the longer the Camry stayed, the more Adrian wondered. At the very least, it confirmed that the meeting at the school had taken place, and the allegations had been aired. He assumed that a statement had by now been made to the police. Interviews would then begin. Mr H would receive a visit because he was the first one Alex told. Next would be Alex's parents. His mother would cry for the second or third time and his father would swear and shout. Eventually, Alex's mates at school would be questioned for evidence or corroboration, especially those in Adrian's English class. They'd be asked what Mr Pomeroy was like as a teacher, what his reputation was among the students. They'd be asked if they witnessed preferential treatment for any particular student, or suspicious behaviour. Of course the students wouldn't tell the police what really went on in the classroom – the stupid shit they did to themselves and each other, a bunch of testosterone-fuelled lads intent on fucking whatever they could get their hands on, or at least thinking and talking about fucking as much as they could.

Adrian got up off the lounge. Nguyet was folding clothes in their bedroom. He stood behind her and put his arms around her, and she relaxed against his chest. He kissed her hair. She put the clothes she was holding on the bed and turned and hugged him and sighed, and he knew what the sigh was for. Over the past two days they'd shown each other more affection than they had for several weeks, if not months. In fact, the marriage had been troubled for over four years but they had somehow found a way to function. It now seemed ironic that the year he first taught Alex was the year their trouble began. The two were not directly connected, of course, but there were perhaps some furtive links. Having entered Adrian's life at that very time, Alex might now bring an end to his marriage.

Now, Adrian thought; *now is the time to tell her*. Even though he knew it would destroy this rare moment.

Then came a knock at the door.

Adrian said he'd get it – he was ready for Bowman – but before he opened the door he saw blue through the opaque glass.

Two officers had come for him, an older woman and a younger man. The female was a senior constable, and the male reminded him of Noel as a first-year officer – young, yet to be appalled by what humanity is fully capable of. Especially against its own. Adrian looked down at the man's left lapel – the plain navy blue of a probationary constable. In the distance over his shoulder, Bowman was leaning against his car bonnet, arms folded, here for the show.

It was then that Adrian understood – and then that he resigned himself to the thought of Noel.

WENDY

'Well, where the fuck is he?'

Simmo didn't know, of course – he was the one who had phoned her. But Wendy felt much better after airing her frustrations with a rhetorical question. Only Noel himself knew where he'd been for most of the afternoon.

This wasn't the first time Simmo had called her mobile to talk about Noel. The first came a bit over a year ago, when he asked if everything was okay in the marriage. Wendy thought it was just Simmo trying it on with her again, so she laughed and said no, nothing was wrong – situation normal. She told Simmo that it was a good try but she still wasn't interested in him, and never would be.

She had said it sympathetically but he'd persisted with all seriousness, saying he had noticed a change in Noel's mentality at work. When Wendy asked what that meant, Simmo just said something 'wasn't quite right with him'. At the time, Wendy had her ideas about why Noel might be distracted from policing, but she didn't feel ready to talk to anyone about Riley. Not yet. She had ended the call by saying she'd keep an eye on Noel – and that she was thankful they had a friend like Simmo to look out for them. For better or for worse, Simmo had been a phone call away for sixteen years.

Wendy and Noel met at the Goulburn Academy when they were in their early twenties. He looked good in uniform, and even better with a gun in his hands on the firing range, though she was a more accurate shot. He was a hard worker in the gym and on the obstacle course, and she helped him get through the study. Noel was the kind of officer other recruits wanted to be stationed with because he was dependable, sturdy. On weekends she sometimes drove him to Canberra to show off her old haunts and stay at her mother's house. She was close to her mother. Noel often spoke about his mother in a respectful way, and this tenderness had ultimately triggered Wendy's love for him.

They served their first couple of years in Kings Cross, sharing a flat in Darlinghurst and then in Randwick. But soon Noel got wind of the opportunities in the west, and eventually talked her into moving to Perth. They got stationed in different suburbs, and one night after work Noel brought his new mate Simmo home for a few drinks. The guy wasn't backward about coming forward, especially when he'd put a few cans away. Wendy vividly recalled Simmo sitting on a stool in their kitchen with a big dumb grin, calling her 'Peaches' and asking about the chances of a threesome. Noel and Simmo thought that was hilarious – they were like a couple of adolescents. Wendy said definitely not.

Perth was good to them. The sense of space they felt, having come from Sydney, made them want to fill it. They got married, had Grace a year later, and then Riley two years after her. Wendy never returned to the force. Motherhood changed her and her priorities. She couldn't fathom the idea of dealing with scumbags all day and then coming home to her girls and reading picture books – the gulf between instilling her children with the wonder of the world and what she witnessed in that world each day on the job was too great. But Noel climbed the ranks and they bought the house in Dianella – a house she despised yet agreed to because Noel was in love with its rigid and covert aesthetics, and she was still in love with Noel. Besides, he was the one bringing home the main income; Wendy was studying occupational therapy part-time at uni and doing a few shifts a week at a cafe.

As the girls grew older, Noel grew quieter. He spoke less and less of his family, and hardly ever rang his mother. He blamed distance and time, but Wendy knew that he had chosen that distance and time. Noel had insisted on Perth not just because of the opportunities but because Sydney was a trap, because the proximity to family was claustrophobic, because he wanted something different for himself. Noel possessed an innate desire to cut and run, she now understood that, and Perth had been an exit sign.

After Simmo's initial call a year ago, he phoned her a couple of times to ask if Noel was around because he couldn't get him on the mobile and no one at the station knew where he was. Wendy told herself not to overthink it. She obeyed. Then came this latest call.

'All I know is that a mate on patrol spotted him heading east past the airport this afternoon,' Simmo said, 'and he's not picking up calls.'

'I know. His mother called with family news and I couldn't get him either.'

Wendy stood at the sliding door to the patio. She tried

to remember where she'd noticed brothels around town but doubted this, like she doubted an affair. Although she couldn't say her own sex life was satisfying, Noel certainly could; he often did.

'What was his mood like before he left the station?'

'He was edgy all day.'

She looked across the yard, at the six-foot aluminium fencing. The sun was almost down and she could faintly hear Grace chatting online with a schoolfriend in her bedroom. *Noel and his fucking walls*, she thought.

'Something's really not right,' Simmo added.

Wendy heard the automatic roller door going up and Noel's car pulling into the garage. 'He's here,' she said. 'I better go.'

She put her mobile on the sideboard and went around the kitchen bench and started on the mushrooms for dinner. Moments later, Noel came in smelling like he'd been smoking all afternoon, wherever he'd been.

'Hello,' she said.

'Hey.'

'You're a bit late.'

He walked straight past her and out to the patio. He asked where the girls were and she told him, trying to focus on the mushrooms so as to not slice herself, but all the while thinking about the old Noel, the husband who rubbed her neck before she knew she needed it, the husband who always said he'd put her before anyone else, the husband who tried to humour her with lame celebrity impersonations, and the father who said he loved his daughters like nothing else in the world. Noel was a good man lost.

'Where've you been?'

Beers with the boys, he lied.

Calm, casual voice, she told herself, then she asked if Simmo was there too.

And Noel said yes. Noel said yeah, Simmo was.

★

When Noel ended the phone call with his mother he placed the mobile down on the patio table. He walked off into the yard, then Wendy heard the side gate latch. He was gone again. Cut and run.

When he returned, Wendy was combing Grace's hair on the lounge, and Riley was sitting in Noel's armchair with knees bent and spread like a guy. Noel entered through the sliding door, said nothing and went down the hall. A minute later Wendy heard the shower.

By the time she'd finished cleaning up and getting the girls to bed, Noel was asleep. The girls – she couldn't help her old ways. The *kids*.

★

Three days later they were on a plane. Wendy and Riley sat beside each other, and Noel and Grace were in the row in front. On take-off, Wendy watched the crown of Noel's head and wondered what the hell was going on in there.

Two days before, he was eating breakfast when he announced he was returning to Sydney. 'I'm going home,' he said. 'I've got plenty of leave.'

To Wendy it had sounded as though he wasn't coming back. 'Good,' she'd said. 'Adrian needs you.'

Noel shook his head. 'Adrian's never needed me.' His

words were full with cereal. She despised the sloppy way he ate sometimes.

'Maybe he didn't in the past, or maybe he just never said so, but he needs you now.'

In a way Wendy was grateful for the turn of events: their marriage needed some kind of change. She was beginning to feel desperate for it, maybe even daring something more for herself. She wondered if the past would provide those needs.

'Have you spoken to him?' she had asked.

He'd said he had tried, but she couldn't help thinking that a lot of what Noel said these days was bullshit. 'He's turned his phone off and shut down his online stuff.'

Fair enough, she thought, *considering the circumstances*.

Wendy had a soft spot for Adrian. She realised a long time ago that she was more prepared to defend Adrian to the hilt than she was Noel. Adrian was simply a nicer person. And she couldn't entertain the idea that the allegations were valid. This punk kid would get what was coming to him.

'Anyway,' Noel had said, 'Mum wants me there so the decision is made.'

There it is, she'd thought. *Noel's allegiance to his mother*. Wendy hadn't seen this in her husband for quite some time, and wondered if returning to the east coast would revive the old Noel. The man she'd fallen in love with.

She then told him she'd book the tickets, and that they would all go. Grace and Riley hadn't been to Sydney for eight years, she said, and the school would be okay about them having a short time away for family reasons. Wendy could get her shifts at the clinic covered. A decent trip would give the kids an appreciation of where Noel grew up – he could show them his childhood house. She knew that would mean a lot to them. And when Wendy had her fill of Pomeroy family drama, she could drive a hire car to Canberra and see her mother. The thought of stealing more time for herself was solidifying.

Riley then came in wearing shorts and a T-shirt. Wendy noticed the chest binding through the material. She didn't know why Riley even needed compression yet – she was still flat-chested enough to look like a boy. Wendy wondered when the request for hormones would come. There'd be a trip to the counsellor before that.

'What's this about?' Riley had said, putting on his best twelve-year-old boy's voice.

Wendy looked Noel in the eye. 'Your uncle and your father.'

TWO

TWO

ADRIAN

'I'm Detective Inspector Fielder,' the officer said, showing Adrian his nametag. He had a low-key voice. Flat. Like he was bored.

Fielder made some notes and glanced up, pointing the end of his biro at Adrian's face. 'That's quite a nose you've got there. Painful?'

Fielder could easily have been Mr H's brother – older and wearier, but with the same kind of moustache. Adrian wondered what it was about men and moustaches. For some reason, being near a moustache made him want to lean over and pull on it.

Adrian looked over at the senior constable, the officer who had brought him in. She was leaning against the wall, keeping an eye on things. 'I manage,' he answered.

'How did it occur?'

He felt like lying. He didn't want to admit that his broken and lacerated nose was the result of a panic attack brought on by this impending event and its series of interrogations. But he also knew that a flurry of unverifiable information would increase their suspicion of his guilt. And contradiction was what he feared most.

'It was a car accident,' he replied. 'I provided a statement.'

'I see,' said Fielder. Then, as if to signify that the pleasantries were over, he leant forward to engage the recording device on the other side of the desk. 'You need to know that this interview is being recorded, okay?' Adrian nodded, and Fielder sat back and arranged his papers.

Adrian looked at the recording device, and then at the camera installed between the ceiling and door. The door had a small window of reflective glass, which he knew people could see through because he'd looked on the way in. It was all very bare and grey. It matched Fielder's tone.

'Are you aware why you've been brought in for this interview today, Mr Pomeroy?'

Adrian watched the digital recorder, its digits ticking over. He rehearsed his response mentally before speaking. 'I believe that Alex Bowman has made allegations against me.'

'That's correct, Mr Pomeroy. Statements have been made alleging aggravated indecent assault by you on a minor, and our first task here is to establish the facts around these allegations. I'm hoping you can assist us with this in the best way possible.'

Adrian guessed this would have been a good time to ask for the union rep, or to contact his lawyer. But he had never joined the union and didn't have a lawyer. He nodded. The less said, the better.

'What is your relationship to Alex Bowman?'

'He's a student in my English class. I taught him in Year Seven and now in Year Eleven.'

'So is it accurate to say that your relationship is on a professional basis only?'

'Yes.'

And no.

'You are his teacher, in a position of authority – correct?'

'Yes.'

And no.

'In your opinion, does that relationship occasionally have cause to extend beyond what might be considered professional?'

'That depends.'

'Please explain.'

'On the student, sir.'

'Continue.'

'Some students need a personal approach in order for the teaching to be effective.'

'And is Alex Bowman a student who you would describe as requiring a more personal approach from your teaching?'

'Yes.'

'And yet you stated a moment ago that the relationship is purely professional. Would you like to correct that response?'

'What I mean is that a personal approach to teaching can be part of my professional role.'

'Then can you describe what you mean by a personal approach, Mr Pomeroy?'

Adrian leant against the back of the chair and put his hands behind his head. He then realised that this was the exact pose of a perpetrator being arrested. He folded his arms across his chest. 'Look, I know what you're trying to get at here, and I know you think I did whatever it is Alex said I did, but—'

'Let me be clear, Mr Pomeroy,' Fielder interrupted. 'I make no assumptions as to whether or not the alleged incidents have occurred. It must be understood that it is not my role to decide your guilt or innocence. My role is to establish the facts. The greatest problem in criminal investigations is the potential for an officer to assume the validity of the alleged victim's statement and then set out to prove that assumption right. I understand that an allegation of indecent assault on a minor has the potential to damage a person's future, whether or not the allegations are factual. Because of this I think it's best for all involved that the facts are established promptly and thoroughly. Do you agree?'

Adrian nodded.

'Now' – Fielder looked down to his notes – 'please describe what you mean by a personal approach, Mr Pomeroy.'

*

Seven months earlier. It was late evening and Adrian was going about the routine of getting Tam to bed. Noo wasn't well – she said there was a burning sensation in her chest, probably indigestion from the red onion in her *goi ga*.

He settled Tam beneath the covers and stroked the boy's straight black hair away from his face. Perhaps it was the half-light, perhaps the evening tone, but whenever he tucked the boy in like this he couldn't help seeing the piccolo face of his son as a toddler. The bath routine was his task back then, and he had always found significance in the event – pouring water over his son's plump little body as he splashed and tipped a full cup into an empty cup and back again. The simplicity of the play brought Adrian remarkable joy. Tam meant *heart* in Vietnamese, and at moments like those Adrian was glad they had chosen no other name.

Nguyet always said Adrian would eat the boy if he could, and while he laughed in agreement it wasn't really like that. He did hunger for the boy's affection, for the contact of his lips on the boy's bright skin, but it was more about proximity – that the small space between them was an intimacy wholly theirs. Unbreached. Still, Adrian sometimes imagined putting the boy's entire body in his mouth, if only to protect him from everything and everyone else out there.

Now, Adrian kissed a line between the boy's forehead and nose, felt the familiar swell in his chest, said goodnight and left the room.

Nguyet was lying on the bed, reading. She said she was trying to distract herself from the feeling in her chest. Adrian offered to go and buy some antacids, and she said she'd appreciate that. He got his keys and wallet and shut the front door behind him.

Adrian liked driving at night, the dashboard lit up like an old arcade game and the street lamps a runway. He'd scroll through the radio stations until he hit upon a sound that paired with his mood – sometimes ambient dance music, sometimes classical piano, sometimes alternative rock. Tonight he discovered a persuasive jazz tune with velvety trumpet and piano that spoke directly to his romantic tendencies.

He wound down the window and put his arm on the sill. It was a cool night but not too fresh – a trace of summer remained in the early autumn. He felt young. He felt like he could drive all night.

Reluctantly he pulled up at the small convenience store where Noo worked, half a dozen blocks from home. He switched off the engine and went in. He walked the aisles quickly but couldn't see what he wanted, so he asked the woman behind the counter, telling her it was for Noo. The woman said no, they didn't stock things like that, and directed him to a chemist in Blacktown, which she thought closed at eight. It was close to eight already, but he knew there was a twenty-four-hour convenience store closer to Parramatta. He thanked the woman and got going.

There was little traffic and he drove without urgency. His thoughts drifted to school and the small incidents of the day – the inconsequential acts and expressions that pass by, noticed but not analysed. He tried to gather them into something meaningful now, but failed, because although he was getting physically closer to the school, his thoughts were moving elsewhere, through time and place, as he passed a street crossing which he knew led directly to the house where he grew up.

That street, that house … He envisaged standing on the driveway and looking, with childhood eyes, through the old timber and wire mesh fence, along the long front yard towards the house. The crumbling wooden letterbox on the gatepost … his mother's rose beds, which he and Noel had to weed each summer. He remembered pushing Noel off his bicycle into one of the rosebushes, and the emotion that ran through him as Noel was carried inside and laid out on the kitchen floor so Glenda could pull out the thorns. He remembered the blood on the lino, and his brother's legs wrapped in gauze. He had felt culpable but not at all remorseful – as far as he was concerned, Noel deserved each and every one of those bloody thorns. He envisaged looking up and down the street to where the twins lived a few doors along on the other side, and to where the old bloke lived who bred budgies and quails. He remembered the time he arrived home to see the one of the housing commission units burning, the black smoke lifting and the fire truck wailing.

His imagination was stepping him along the driveway towards the carport and the house, an old weatherboard job with brown trim and front windows that reminded him of a face, the eyes lidded by venetian blinds. But as he walked into the convenience store, the fluoro lights erased his musing. He checked the aisles absent-mindedly, forgetting even what he was there for, when he stopped in the middle of an aisle and looked around at the shelves of confectionery.

Someone was behind him.

'Sir?'

He turned to the young store attendant, and for a moment thought he was back at school, though he didn't know why. Then the moment passed into recognition – of course he knew the face, just not in this context. 'Akker?'

'Good to see you, sir.'

'I didn't know you worked here.'

Akker looked down at his badge, the polo shirt with the logo, his black jeans. 'I haven't been here long. About two months.'

'Not that I come here often or anything. You like the work?'

He looked around. 'It's okay. The money helps my family.' He straightened some packets on a shelf. 'It's a bit boring but I like working at night. The night's good. Quiet.'

The boy was being more conversational than he was in class.

'You must get some interesting characters in here at night.'

He smiled, nodded. 'You live near here?' Akker asked.

'I wouldn't say near, no.'

'What are you here for?'

Adrian caught himself, and tracked his thoughts back to earlier in the evening and Noo on the bed. 'Antacids, actually. Just some antacids.'

'For your wife?'

Adrian nodded.

'What's she like?'

'Sorry?'

'What's her name – what's she like? You don't ever talk about her at school.'

'Well, school is for education on topics other than my wife.'

Akker shut up then. Another customer walked into the store.

'Those antacids?'

Akker showed him to the right section. The products were on a low shelf, so Adrian had to crouch. Akker stood behind him while Adrian looked at the products – tablets, liquids, chewables. The black jeans brushed his shoulder – a knee perhaps. The boy was almost standing over him as he made his choice and, next thing, Adrian felt a hand come down onto his shoulder, a flat palm with fingers wrapping the curve of muscle. It was a gentle placement, almost a caress. Like Akker didn't know if he should be doing this but wanted to do it anyway.

Adrian turned his head a little but said nothing: he didn't know what to say. He felt the heat of the hand through his shirt, an intimacy altogether unexpected, then grabbed whatever packet and stood, and the hand let go. Within a minute Adrian had paid and left. Nothing was said. No eye contact.

Adrian drove the most direct route home. He switched off the radio because he needed the headspace to replay those few seconds in his mind. Akker hadn't needed to stand so close. And the hand – Adrian felt Akker's palm for the rest of the drive, as though flesh could burn. Regardless of how he tried to distract himself, the sensation persisted, even after he arrived home to find Noo asleep on top of the bedsheets, still in her clothes.

As he carefully undressed her and folded her body into bed, he told himself that nothing was meant by the gesture – that it was just a friendly thing, that the kid was probably unaware of the personal space he'd breached. As he poured himself a glass of wine and sat on the front porch, he wondered why he was even giving so much thought to what had happened. Eventually he concluded that Alex was simply reaching out – literally and figuratively – and that it was his role as a teacher to recognise the boy's needs and respond accordingly. Drinking his wine, Adrian told himself that Alex Bowman was indeed a quality student who hadn't yet reached his potential, a boy who would benefit from a more personal teaching approach.

Yeah, he thought, *that's the phrase.*

And as he put the empty wine glass on the kitchen sink and took himself to bed, reaching for the warmth of the body beside him, he reminded himself that he had not touched the boy – the boy had touched him.

The boy is not an object of my desire, he told the night, and decided that he needn't think more about it. *I am in full control.* He knew, however, that neither statement was a complete and verifiable truth.

★

'Mr Pomeroy, one of the witnesses described you as being inquisitive about students' private lives. Now, in a boys' school I assume that sexuality is a topic raised on various occasions, both formally and informally. Are you of the opinion that you became more involved with the private life of the alleged victim than your employment required?'

Adrian read between the lines but he wanted Fielder to just come out and say it. 'Sorry, I don't follow your meaning.'

'What I'm asking is whether or not the alleged victim's

sexual persuasion ever became a topic of discussion between you and the alleged victim.'

So someone had said he was inquisitive ... Well, yes, it was true enough, and he was sorry. He'd gone and stuck his nose in Akker's business with no right to do so. He hadn't put his nose there to get his hands on Akker or Akker's hands on him, but that was now a moot point.

He had seen too much. For some reason the students always thought that because the focus was on him at the front of the room, only they were watching him – but he saw each of them in great detail too. And the detail was revealing. Every day he was audience to a private demonstration of youth on show, with all the usual players. Villains, jesters, scribes, tragic heroes. All the big themes were there: pride and the abuse of power; the fraught relationship between men and the gods; crimes committed by heroes who cannot see their own folly until the world collapses around them ... Probably the comparison was over the top but it allowed him to maintain a sense of humour – and entertaining yourself was sometimes the only way to get through a day in the classroom. Sad but true.

Marley was the cruel jester of Year Eleven English. He was a solid lump of a kid, almost arrogant in his physical presence, leaning over the table half the time or lounging back in his chair, with a mouth that followed. Whenever Adrian asked about a concept or a theme, Marley was the one to shout something mildly provocative. Early in the year Adrian was talking about Chekhov and the potency of the right word to strike the reader's heart.

'Is that like what's on the door in the toilets, sir?' Marley said.

Adrian looked up from his book. 'I'm not interested in that, Marley.'

'But it's exactly what you mean, sir. It's true.'

'Yes, I'm sure it is, Marley.'

For some reason this made Marley ecstatic. He could barely remain in his chair.

'So it is true you take it up the arse, sir?'

The boys all laughed, of course, and Marley turned to Akker beside him, seeking approval with a fist bump. Akker hesitated, looking sheepish, then bumped him back.

Adrian had visualised physically harming Marley on several occasions, but the closest he ever came to that was during lunchtime duty on the oval, where the boys exacted physical distress on each other by playing tackle football. Adrian was supposed to stop this kind of activity but he always let it ride. He gained a certain pleasure from watching this culturally acceptable form of brutalisation, the contest of force as the boys grew into their shoulders, their chests, and hammered the hell out of each other. They always thanked him for his leniency – which was the only leniency they afforded him.

But sexuality and masculine potency were sites of contest from the first to the final bell. The boys were suspect of anyone who strayed from heteronormative behaviour and yet didn't comprehend the irony of some of their own actions. Whenever he tried to get the boys to do some creative writing they said writing was for poofters. He tried to get them to write about social media; once he even tried to get them to text lines of prose to each other, to compose a group short story, but that devolved as soon as a picture of someone's genitals did the rounds. Akker – God, Akker – was one of the only ones who didn't join in.

Adrian still had hope in the boy back then. He thought there

was enough of Alex and Alex's sensibilities left in Akker to keep
him above the idiocy. He had hoped the boy would become a
writer, or a humanist of some description, and if not in vocation
then at least in the small acts of the everyday. He'd hoped for so
much, and none of it for himself but for the boy. He'd hoped …

But no. There was never any explicit conversation about
Akker's sexual proclivities. Being explicit isn't needed when the
implicit makes a more potent statement.

'I'm sorry, Detective Fielder, but I can't recall a single
occasion when Alex and I spoke on that topic.'

'Do you admit that there was a change in the professionally
established relationship earlier this year?'

'That's not untrue.'

'Who initiated that change in the relationship?'

'He did.'

Fielder was becoming more animated. 'Mr Pomeroy, can you
provide any evidence to support that claim?'

Evidence. Adrian suddenly realised that officers would be
waltzing through his front door right now, seizing materials
and equipment. The box of unfinished marking, his work diary,
his desktop and notebook computers, his mobile. Neighbours
would witness his stuff being shut into the trunks of police
vehicles and driven away. And then there was Noo. While they
were carting out the stuff, she'd be standing back and wondering
what was going on. His only hope was that she might be out
picking up Tam from school.

A digital forensics team had perhaps already begun plugging
in his gear and hacking the hard drives, retrieving his search
engine history, scrolling through his text messages and call log
and email and social media, copying and pasting into folders

on their own databases and filing records. Or something like that. He didn't know much about the law but he knew the police would be well within their rights to seize and detain his possessions. His personal life would be prised open. A profile was being built, but it was not of him, exactly – it was of Adrian Pomeroy the Kiddie Fiddler, Adrian Pomeroy the Divorced, Adrian Pomeroy the Shamed, the Incarcerated, the Sodomised. It was Adrian Pomeroy the Utterly Broken.

These were the thoughts rushing through his mind as Fielder looked at his papers and waited for a response. 'Do you need me to repeat the question, Mr Pomeroy?'

'Sorry,' he said. *Stop apologising.* 'Yes, I think I do.'

'Is there any evidence to substantiate your claim that any change in the relationship was initiated by Mr Bowman?'

'There is.'

★

Two days after seeing Akker in the convenience store, Adrian received an email from a sender called *godhand*. It was the weekend and he'd been up late marking essays, and decided to check his email before packing it in for the night. When he opened his email account the message sat there at the top of his inbox, boldly begging. At first he assumed it was spam and hovered a finger over delete, but the subject line got his attention: 'you have been touched'.

Akker …

For two days Adrian had avoided thinking about Akker's gesture. Still, the fact that he knew he'd avoided thinking about it also meant that it was a thought to be had in the first place, and this implied not avoidance but something far more terrifying – denial. But now, with the appearance of the email, he was suddenly aware of the emotional upwelling he had suppressed. Akker was indeed touching him. The fucker was trying to get under his skin, but what his true intentions were, Adrian could only speculate.

The email had no content other than an attachment with the file name *teacher*. He hesitated, listening for where Noo was in the house, then double-clicked.

What followed was a story about a young man. He is on all fours like a dog, naked, his wrists and ankles bound, his palms and knees in dirt. There is a block of wood between his thighs and another one supporting his chest. The blocks are there to keep him in this position, with his face and hair hanging forward. A man walks around the boy, kicking dirt in his face, saying that the dog's crime is denial of what he knows to be true. The man spits on his back, and the dog feels each spit blaze against his skin like a foreshadowing of the coming event. To hide was his crime; to burn alive is his punishment.

Another man gathers wood from nearby and stacks it for a pyre. But this man is different: he's not there to punish. He has another role to play. And as he walks back and forth, loading and unloading armfuls of wood, he steals glances at the boy. He smiles, and the boy thinks he knows why: this man is here not to throw his body onto the fire, but to liberate him. The man will do this for two reasons: first, because he is the one who caused the boy to be here in the dirt, awaiting hellfire; and second, because the boy knows in his heart that the man loves him. From the description of this man, it is clear he is a rendering of Adrian.

There are other characters, too, watching from the windows

of houses. Some are shouting, others crying. But these people are of no consequence, for by the time the wood has been stacked the sun is low in the west and it has grown bigger, and somehow hotter, and somehow brighter. This light has an intensity beyond the sun – it is light from a source far more formidable, and like a star entering the atmosphere, it burns brighter and closer with each passing moment. 'It is God Himself,' someone calls out, and the people in the houses move away from the windows. The spitting man kneels in the dirt and begins to pray. The boy is laughing now: he was the one to be burned and yet he is now calm, almost serene, while all others are in fear of the coming fire, their eyes closed against the light, which has become unbearable.

Then the boy feels a hand against his skin. It is a warm hand, a familiar hand, and the hand knows his body well. The hand finds the boy's hands and a knife is brought through the bindings around his wrists and ankles. The wood blocks are removed and the boy feels himself being lifted, then carried.

When the light returns to normal, the people come out of the houses and the spitting man stops praying. They all look to the sky to see the comet streak towards the horizon. They then turn to see the boy in the dirt, but he is gone – riding, they believe, on the tail of the comet.

★

Fielder's moustache undulated with his mouth and he sat forward. 'What kind of evidence are we talking about?'

'He sent me emails, suggestive stories,' Adrian said. 'They might prove something.'

Fielder looked at his colleague and wrote a note. 'Good,' he

said, then he stood and picked up his papers. 'Can I get you
something to drink? Coffee?'

'Is this going to take much longer?'

'That depends.' Fielder pushed in his chair and looked at the
recording device, which was still ticking over, then at Adrian.

'On what?'

'On you, Mr Pomeroy. Do you have anything else you can
tell me which will assist the investigation?'

Adrian thought about this. Fielder was opening a door for
Adrian, or at least leaving it unlocked. But then again, perhaps
Fielder was only presenting the illusion of escape – the offer
of a drink seemed to contradict the suggestion that Adrian was
in control of how much longer he'd have to sit in that chair.
No, Fielder knew there was more story to tell. Adrian certainly
knew there was more, without a doubt, but he worried about
the supposed 'facts' and how they were stacking up – what
shape they were creating. How Fielder was putting them
together in his notebook and the story Adrian believed he was
telling were inevitably different, because there were only so
many 'facts' which could be reported. In this way the whole
enterprise was ludicrous. Dates, locations – these things could
be objectively reported; but descriptions of actions, intentions,
thought processes and contextual circumstances – these were
the subjectivities which would come to define or destroy
him if the case progressed. The more of these subjectivities he
presented, the more complex the story would become, and he
assumed there was some kind of tipping point, a point of no
return where his only option was full disclosure – or as full as he
could articulate. He believed he hadn't yet arrived at that tipping
point. He believed he was still in control.

Yet there was more he could tell, for now. There was still a chance to cut this off, right here and right now. There was still a chance to deny Akker the goal towards which, Adrian now understood, he'd been working for the best part of the school year. Ever since the series of unfortunate events went one step too far.

Adrian made up his mind. He looked at the senior constable, then at Fielder. 'Yes,' he said. 'I can tell you more.'

ALEX

While Alex's mum wanted him to be a believer, he only wanted someone to believe in him. Someone in the flesh, not a god. But this person could not be his father.

Alex liked working on his vocabulary. When he came across a word he didn't recognise, he fished it from his dictionary and made note of it, repeating the definition under his breath until it sank in. Doing this had helped his reading and writing, especially in his first year of high school, but when it came to describing his dad his vocabulary was limited to words like *prick* and *arsehole*. Because Danny often was a prick, especially to Alex, who was a passive kid who did what was asked of him and tried to please. But Alex's weakness was his mouth – he just couldn't help a cheeky crack here or there, pointing out something that he felt was too important or true to leave unsaid.

Danny always got the shits with that. 'You and your fucken mouth,' he'd say. 'You watch your lip, son.'

And when Alex didn't watch it, Danny's belt came off. 'Pull your pants down and touch your toes,' Danny would say, and if Alex flinched he got double. Sometimes Danny even told him to go and choose a belt from the cupboard – the softer the leather and the wider the strap, he worked out, the better. He also learned that tensing his bum cheeks lessened the sting. Shannon copped it too, so Alex shared his tips with her, and told her to be strong and imagine the day they were old enough that he wouldn't be able to do it to them anymore. That was what Alex thought of whenever he was leaning over the bed, exposed, expecting. The word *hate* came easily during those times.

But Alex knew that reducing his father to a belt-wielding prick wasn't entirely fair. Alex was empathetic enough to know that things were always more complicated – that actions were most often the result of a complex series of events. And while Alex didn't know exactly what made his dad tick, he knew enough to give him the benefit of the doubt, even if it sometimes meant more disappointment and hurt. Part of this was due to the fact that when he looked at his dad he saw a projection of himself – the same sandy skin, blond hair, angular features.

In your hand are power and might, and in your hand it is to make great and to give strength to all. Alex read this on the plaque at church whenever his mum got the family motivated enough to go. They weren't devout followers, but his parents liked the idea that, whenever they attended, the family were more respectable. The truth, Alex knew, was that Danny couldn't give a flying fuck about religion – Michaela was the one pushing for the family's salvation.

Michaela called Danny her 'diamond in the rough', and just how rough he'd been came to light one day when an old mate showed up on their doorstep with beer and rum. The two guys sat together in the lounge and talked about the Westmead they'd grown up in – about the commission housing and the boys they'd go tagging with, the minor break-ins they'd pulled, mainly of cars, derelict shops, empty houses. About sniffing glue and inhaling butane. About nights out on cheap bourbon, and about smoking joints laced with acid. It was at that point Michaela told Alex and Shannon to go to bed, but Alex had listened from the hallway, curious about what this old friend was revealing about his father.

They talked about the poofter-bashing hunts they went on, about trailing guys walking near the public toilets in Parramatta Park, and the time they caught two faggots in the act: they shoved them to the grass, a couple of the boys pinning them down while another spray-painted 'homo' across their backs and stuck sticks up their arses. Danny and his mate laughed the whole way through that story. Then there was the turf war with the Lebs, and how one of them had pulled a gun on Danny outside the Westfield.

What Danny didn't talk about that night was how he'd got it on at a party with a Lebanese girl who turned out to be a sister of one of the Leb Boys, and how the Leb Boys had bashed him when they found out, breaking his jaw and fracturing his skull. Alex knew this because his mum had told him. Danny then moved to his uncle's house in Port Macquarie, which was where he'd met Michaela. That was when his life's momentum changed, and he learned that people could be kind, and that he could also be kind if he chose to.

Michaela had also told the kids the story of how she and Danny had met – how his uncle got him a job driving a delivery truck for a farm supplies store her family used to buy from.

'I used to eye off all the delivery boys,' she told them, 'but the day he drove onto our land was the day I knew to stop looking.'

They went out for a few months and eventually moved into a duplex in town. Danny held onto his job and Michaela continued to work for her parents on their small produce farm.

'We never agreed on anything,' she laughed, 'which I thought was sweet at the time.'

They married during a drought year. When the dry really set in, the work dried up too, so Danny convinced her to move to Sydney's west. They lived with Danny's parents in the old house for a while, getting by on the dole, until Danny got back into the trucking business and they saved enough for a rental bond. Then Alex came along, and Shannon two years later.

As the children grew and the family moved to a larger house, Danny took on a cleaning job to bring in more cash, which meant his family saw him less and less. He didn't complain much, but the hours took their toll, and working day and night meant that he got next to no sleep. Drinking came easily, and so did anger – he'd bang the bedroom wall and shout at the kids when they played loudly. And when he belted the kids he said it wasn't him punishing them but them punishing themselves, which always made Alex think about the saying on the plaque at church – about God's hand having power and might, just like his dad's, and maybe like he'd have one day.

Michaela would hug him after each belting. 'He only does these things because he loves you,' she'd say, and for a while he believed her.

By the time Alex was twelve and at high school, he was looking for someone who recognised his potential, someone who could open his mind to all that was possible in the world.

He clearly recalled the day he came home with his first Year Seven report. He showed it to his mum after dinner was done and she was washing up. His achievement across most subjects was above average, and the comments from his teachers were glowing, but his best result was in English.

'What's that?' Danny called from the lounge room.

'Alex's school report,' she said. 'He's done really well in English.'

'English?' Danny said. 'So he should – he's probably the only kid at that school who speaks it at home.'

Michaela then read out Mr Pomeroy's comments. She put her arm around her son. 'Says he's got a talent for storytelling,' she called to Danny.

Alex thought of Mr Pomeroy – his true teacher. A light to follow.

'That'd be right. Bullshit artist in the making.'

'It's reading and writing,' Alex said. 'Writing stories is the best part.'

'Yeah, well, writing stories won't put food in anyone's belly, will it? Just think about that.'

Alex didn't want to think about that. Maybe later, when he had a family of his own, but not now. 'Yes, Dad.'

'And this teacher who says he wants to nurture you – you can tell him that if he wants to hear a real man's story, I can tell him mine.'

'Yes, Dad.'

But he told Mr Pomeroy no such thing, for he already felt love for his teacher. More love, he quickly decided, than what he'd ever felt for his own father. Not that anyone knew. Alex tucked this adoration inside his mind and heart, though even back then he had begun to explore his feelings through the stories he wrote for class. Throughout the year, they became more and more of an outlet, and he looked to Mr Pomeroy for some clue that he had read between the lines of those stories and understood what was there but not there. Those traces of his sentiments, like a message written in lemon juice. And while Mr Pomeroy made no acknowledgement, Alex believed that something was developing between them.

On occasion, his adoration edged into another feeling, this kind more physical. He knew what it was to have a crush, but this wasn't some short-lived and meaningless thing. The boys in class had crushes on girls from other schools because of the perfume they wore or how thick their lips were, or because of the way their bums looked when they walked, but this was different. Alex thought of Mr Pomeroy throughout the day and imagined being near him, hearing him talk up close, so close they could share breath, and share knowledge of things far beyond Alex's experience. Sometimes he dared to imagine what it would feel like to touch his teacher – his fingers coming down on Mr Pomeroy's arm or shoulder, or his thigh. These thoughts were enough back then to send Alex into a storm of longing and increasing doubt – doubt that these developing impulses were normal for a twelve-year-old boy, who he knew should be thinking about footy and girls and whatever.

When Alex learned that Mr Pomeroy's name was Adrian, he wrote *AP* in black texta on the underside of his pencil case. One day the boy next to him in English saw the initials and asked who AP was. 'Mr Pomeroy's name is Adrian,' the boy said.

Alex flushed red and shook his head. 'Didn't know that,' he said. 'AP's this girl at church, one of my sister's friends.' He then added, 'She's got huge tits.'

He felt proud of his imaginative rescue, but at the same

time humiliated by the realisation that what had been a private preoccupation could become a public shame. At that moment, Alex Bowman knew he had everything to fear and one thing to hide.

NOEL

When Noel had the urge again so soon, he knew he was done for. He'd barely arrived in Sydney and already he was looking around, wondering if and when and where he could do another burn.

They'd touched down, reclaimed their baggage, waited at the hire car desk and were now on the M5. They'd be on the motorway for a while before turning north to Homebush, and then on to Merrylands, and the whole way would be nothing but traffic and buildings and people walking the tired concrete paths of the city Noel had begun to wonder if he'd ever get back to. Yet here he was – and here he wished he wasn't. The only pleasure he could take from being back was the realisation that he'd changed in his years in the west: Perth felt like home. He was surprised it'd taken him until now, driving with all these other bullshit cars to bullshit places, to realise it. *Jesus*, he thought, *I shouldn't be wasting my time on grass and scrub when this whole joint should be burned to the fucken ground.*

'Do we drive through the city?'

Riley, with her pretend boy's voice. He looked in the rear-vision mirror. 'Nup,' he said.

'No, we're heading west, darling. Your father's family live in the western suburbs.'

Wendy, on her best behaviour. She'd be his rock over the coming week, as long as she stuck around and didn't take off to Canberra to see her mum, the widow turned spinster. Noel couldn't fathom why the old bag never tried to meet another bloke after Wendy's father died all those years ago. Perhaps he just didn't have the heart for that kind of empathy.

Wendy hadn't mentioned Canberra but the idea must've passed through her head. He didn't want to raise it, just in case she'd convinced herself that spending time with his family was more important. After all, seeing his family was what they'd come here to do – why they'd spent all that money on flights instead of on a camping trip near Katherine. Although he was the one who said he'd come back, the girls and Wendy coming along had turned the event into something else. Was this about Adrian? Or the girls? Or was it for Glenda's sake? The notion of just spending time in the company of family had become a perplexing one for Noel. If he didn't feel as though he was getting something out of it, he became resentful, and he didn't want that this time around – he wanted to make this about him, too. Sydney was not only his childhood home but the source of a certain unrest, which he had hoped would die in this shithole the moment he left for Perth. Leaving the past behind and all that. But his unrest had packed itself in his suitcase and shifted into a Perth closet. Ever since then it had morphed into something closer to self-reproach.

Noel looked about the dinky hire car at his girls. Riley had her headphones on, watching the streets fly by. Grace was on her phone. Wendy was tuning the radio to taste.

His wife didn't know the depth of his self-reproach. No one knew. Not even that dickhead service counsellor could get it out of him – the one who didn't last long, and after he got the sack was picked up for possession. Noel was there when the bloke was brought in, all scruffy in filthy jeans and thongs and a bloodied T-shirt. Coked out of his brain, with a baggy in his pocket which a couple of kids had tried to thieve from him at a shopping mall; they'd ended up in a scuffle. Trolley-pushing old ladies were terrified. Clerks watched in awe. Teenagers filmed it with their phones and someone called the cops. The kids got away, leaving the counsellor on the polished floor holding his mouth, teeth busted through a lip. So the arresting officers said.

Noel first met the counsellor as protocol after a colleague was bashed during a pub call-out. Noel never trusted the prying bastard. He kept pressing Noel to spill his guts but Noel reckoned the joker had done some spilling himself – he could tell an alcoholic a mile off, a special ability his dad had blessed him with. Exposure becomes knowledge, eventually. Noel had wondered if the counsellor might've occasionally chucked in a little something extra with the drink, because when you're loose you might as well let it all go and get fucken frayed, right? That kind of thing. Noel had seen it plenty. He knew the kind. The counsellor's eyes blurted out the only thing worse than disinterest, and that was self-interest.

Wendy had found her radio station and now put her hand on Noel's thigh, but her face was turned to the window. Casual affection, not the full commitment. He got it, because Noel found it difficult to fully trust anyone, which gave Simmo the shits, and probably Wendy too. He recognised something seething in her lately but wasn't interested enough to goad the issue out into daylight.

Noel was like that: reliable yet guarded, there but not really there. He never let anyone get closer than arm's length, and truly thought that this was the best way to be, because less input equated to less output. Less investment meant less to lose.

Wendy seemed to be playing that way now too. She wouldn't win, though, Noel knew, because he had perfected the art to the point he now believed he had nothing left to lose.

★

They pulled up at the Merrylands house. They got out of the car and Noel walked around it to open the boot.

'We'll get the suitcases later,' Wendy said. 'Say hello first.' She put her arms around Grace and Riley and walked up the driveway.

Noel hadn't moved.

'I said just leave the bags, darling.'

'It's okay,' he replied. 'You head in with the girls.'

Riley mumbled something but he ignored her.

'Why aren't you coming in?' Wendy asked.

'I need a smoke, don't I?'

There were 'No smoking' stickers on the dash and glove box in the hire car, and the clerk had specifically pointed out the clause in the contract.

Wendy shook her head and embraced Glenda, who'd come out to the driveway. Glenda hugged the girls and touched Grace's hair, saying nice things to them all. She looked over at Noel and smiled.

'I'll be there in a minute, Mum.'

She nodded. 'Love you,' she said.
'Love you too.'
'I'm so glad you made it.'
Noel nodded, though he wasn't so sure.

ADRIAN

One tap. That meant teeth.

'Stop using your teeth. More lip and tongue. Remember?'

The instructions were simple and never changed, yet he got it wrong most times. He was just a boy, after all. Adrian often fails to comprehend this fact, but regardless of how complex the issue of what they were doing could become, the boy's age was the simplest and most essential truth.

Adrian appreciates this more now than he could at the time, and with that appreciation comes the hurt. At that age, the boy was not to blame. But how can Adrian tell him that? There is no way he can go back and tell the boy those things now. If there was guilt, and he wondered why there had to be so much guilt, then he would tell the boy it was not his to keep. That any guilt should be outed, replaced by another emotion. The only problem is that Adrian has no conception of what that other emotion should be.

'Open your mouth wider. Make it bigger. Yeah, that's it. That's good.'

In retrospect, each action appears inevitable. That's how Adrian sees it now. One action led to another, and to another, and so on until the final act. And of course there was desire. What began as a set of specific instructions had quickly turned into a want. A craving, perhaps, by the end, by the time he took the boy in his mouth for the final time.

How did it end? It ended because it had to. There was nothing more to it, really.

Two taps – that was how it ended. Two taps. That meant someone was coming.

'Oh, shit. Move away. Someone's coming!'

★

The interview wore on. Fielder managed to maintain a bored tone, slouching in his seat like some cocky kid at school. Like he was enjoying the process now, tapping the side of his coffee cup with a pen. The sound was beginning to grate on Adrian, who wondered if this was the bad cop routine.

'Mr Pomeroy, do you believe an alleged victim places himself at risk by reporting an incidence of sexual misconduct by his teacher?'

'Yes, of course he does.'

'And what do you suppose those risks are?'

'Victimisation from his peers, perhaps. Embarrassment, ridicule. He'd be the subject of jokes and pranks and gossip, stuff like that. I know the teachers would be wary. He'd probably have to go to a new school.'

'So would you agree that the costs are high?'

Adrian nodded.

'And yet you claim that the only contact you shared outside of the professional relationship involved some emails and suggestive stories. That's not a strong basis for such an allegation, which the student would've known would activate a police investigation and affect his social interactions and schoolwork.'

Adrian said nothing.

'Do you see why I'm struggling to understand the nature of this case, Mr Pomeroy?'

Still nothing.

'You should bear in mind that I have witness accounts and a detailed statement from the alleged victim, which contradict some of the claims you've made so far in this interview. Students claim that you favoured him in class, that you made eyes at him and other subtle sexual advances. That you asked him to stay back after class.'

Adrian took his water and tried to sip but his hands were shaking. He put the glass back on the table.

Fielder watched closely, made a note in his notebook. 'This must be distressing for you too, Mr Pomeroy.'

'Course it is.' His nose throbbed beneath the bandage.

'I can only imagine what's going through your head right now. Would you care to enlighten me? Or would you prefer that I keep using my imagination?'

They were entering the guts of the interview process now, Adrian could see. Things were about to get mucky. He had to fight or flee.

'You know, my brother's a cop,' he began.

'Is that right.'

'Want to know why he became a cop?'

Fielder's moustache said he didn't want to play.

'He didn't have the imagination to be anything else.'

A smile came out from behind Fielder's moustache. He

turned to the senior constable and she smiled as well. Touché. The tension broke. Fielder picked up his pen again and waited until his smile receded. 'Okay, then, let's revisit the email correspondence. Would you say you encouraged or discouraged this activity?'

Adrian knew it could be said he'd encouraged the boy, but he believed no evidence existed – he had never replied to Akker's emails. He wasn't that imprudent.

'Neither,' he said, but he was guilty of both.

Fielder tapped his cup again. 'Of course, you know that hard evidence isn't required if there are sufficient statements discounting the credibility of your claim at trial.'

'I understand.'

'So are you claiming you did nothing at all in response to Alex Bowman's written provocations?'

'I'm not saying I did nothing at all. All I'm saying is that I believe I didn't actively encourage or discourage him.'

'But you did respond in some way.'

'Obviously. Wouldn't you? If I'm guilty of anything, then I'm guilty of responding.'

Fielder leant forward, raised one eyebrow. 'And what was your response, exactly?'

★

Following the first email, a coy game of hide-and-seek began.

The change in Akker's classroom behaviour was subtle – a looseness in the way he sat in his chair, an upturn along the line of his mouth, an intensity of eye contact. Characteristics only Adrian would notice from the front of the room. At first he was confident of his deduction, but over the course of several lessons, when he should have been thinking about a William Golding novel, he became distracted by the thought that perhaps these subtleties were not of Akker's making but his own – that what he found was the result of what he sought.

After a week, this thought became a belief that *godhand* wasn't Akker at all, that the timing of Akker touching him in the convenience store and then receiving the email was pure coincidence. That the description of the man stacking the pyre was not him. He wondered too if the email could have been written by another student, someone blindsiding him, so he began to scrutinise not only Akker's behaviour but that of all his pupils. Each gesture became a sign. Each whispered word on a boy's lips was his name, and a wish for what that boy would like to do with him. Over two weeks, each lesson became a portent.

Then came the second email, and with it the second story.

This story was less abstract than its predecessor, though nonetheless remarkable. It described what could be seen through a window at night: a teacher sits at his desk in his study, marking papers. The light is low. There is no sound. Somewhere else in the house are a woman and a child, but they are so far off in the teacher's mind that they almost do not exist – their presence bleeds into soft furnishings; the woman's body hangs in a cupboard, no more than an empty dress; the child's play becomes a drawing on a sheet of paper, left on the carpet in another room. The teacher finishes his marking and puts his pen aside. He rubs his eyes, stretches, massages his neck with palms and fingertips. He moves the pile of marked papers to the end of the desk and turns to his keyboard and computer screen.

When Adrian read this description he couldn't help but

look out his window; the description was so accurate to his own study that he felt a tremor of vulnerability. He felt exposed, not just physically, but emotionally.

The teacher opens his emails and sees an email from someone called *godhand*. There is a story attached. One about a boy and a depiction of the teacher stacking a pyre. The teacher reads the story, and is described as having his eyes opened to a truth about himself he would rather ignore. But that is difficult. He knows who *godhand* is, and as he sits at his desk he imagines the boy writing the story and thinking of him, and in this exchange a connection is formed. The teacher's thoughts are full with the boy. Sitting in his study chair, he imagines that he and the boy are in the classroom, and there is no one else. The school day has ended and they can now begin what they both want. And as the teacher imagines this scene he grows hard, coaxed by his fingertips. Even though he would prefer to deny it, he can't help it. The knowledge is written in his skin. It surges in his blood, and his blood is full with the boy. So full he could choke.

*

The next day Adrian asked Akker to hang back after class.

'Sir?' he said as he approached. Adrian was rubbing the last hour's work from the whiteboard.

'When's your next shift at the store?'

'Tomorrow night. Why?'

'What time do you finish?'

'Nine. But why?'

'Good. I'll see you then,' Adrian said, and put the whiteboard eraser on his desk. He refused eye contact.

Akker nodded, then shifted his bag on his shoulder.

Adrian looked up only as the boy left the room.

★

'Mr Pomeroy, when was the last time you smoked marijuana?'

'I don't recall.'

'But you do smoke, or have smoked, marijuana?'

'I don't see how this relates to the allegations.'

'Okay, then. Where were you on the night of Thursday the eleventh of August?'

'I don't recall specifically. I imagine I was at home with my wife and child.'

'Would it assist your memory if you looked at your work diary?'

'Probably not. It's just got work stuff in it.'

'So you have no recollection of your possible movements or activities that night?'

'No. None. Why?'

'I have a statement putting you in the back car park of the convenience store at which the alleged victim was working on the night of Thursday the eleventh of August. It was here that the alleged sexual incident took place in your vehicle. You were reported to be wearing black jeans and a grey jacket, and were possibly under the influence of illicit drugs. We've obtained clothing matching these descriptions from your premises. We've also obtained your vehicle from the wrecking yard. It's been impounded for evidence collection. You should also be aware that we're currently in the process of securing CCTV footage from the convenience store, so if you were there on that night then it's reasonable to assume we will have evidence to prove it.'

'He's saying it happened in the car park?' Had he seen a security camera at the rear of the building?

'Correct. Does that surprise you, Mr Pomeroy?'

This had gone far enough. 'Nothing happened when we were at the car park.'

Fielder looked at the senior constable. Like Adrian had just fucked up.

'But you were in the car park that night?'

'Yes.'

'In your vehicle?'

'Yes.'

'And you invited the alleged victim into your vehicle?'

Stupidly … 'Yes.'

★

It was a couple of minutes to nine when Adrian pulled up in the car park behind the store. He went around to the front of the building but didn't enter, just watched Akker through the window. He was tidying his till, bagging excess coins and neatening eftpos receipts. When he closed the till he saw Adrian through the glass. The kid pulled his signature smirk.

A guy in his fifties then walked past Adrian to enter the store. He and Akker said something to each other, and both glanced at Adrian. Akker shook his head, laughed. *It's all good*, he seemed to be saying. The older guy removed his jacket and put it on the counter, then swapped with Akker at the register, hitting keys on the screen. Akker then came out of the store with his school backpack, and he and Adrian began walking.

'In my car,' Adrian said. 'Out the back.'

There was a dull street lamp at the corner of the car park

driveway, but still plenty of shadow play as they opened the front doors and got into the car. Adrian knew the risk of what he was doing, but he was deaf to his own alarm bells, the warning sirens, his body alerting him of imminent danger. Akker sitting in the passenger seat – where his wife always sat – was sufficient proof. The boy's legs disappearing into the footwell, his chest across the width of the backrest, his right hand on the black of his work trousers. For a moment Adrian felt remorseful that he'd brought the two of them to this scenario, but then reminded himself that it was Akker who had triggered this sequence of events. Adrian was here to rectify this ridiculous situation. He had to shut it down before it went any further – and he knew they could both easily take it further. He wanted to protect Akker as much as himself.

'What's happening, sir? Is there something we need to talk about?'

'Cut the *sir* crap, Akker. We both know what's going on here.'

'I don't know what you mean.'

'Who's coming to pick you up?'

'My mum, but only when I text her that I'm ready. I haven't texted yet.'

'Good. Gives us time.'

'Time to do what, sir?'

'Talk. Just talk.'

'Is that all?'

Akker relaxed back into the seat now, but Adrian didn't want him to get too comfortable.

'Akker, I know you've been to my house.'

'Don't know what you're talking about.'

'I think you do.'

'Why would you think that?'

'Godhand?'

'What's that supposed to mean?'

'You tell me.'

Akker got his phone out of his pocket. The screen lit his face.

'Stop fucking about, Akker. I know you wrote those stories. It couldn't be anyone else. And the way you described my study was too close to be coincidence. You've been around to my fucking house, looking in through my windows, haven't you?'

Akker put the phone between his legs. Light shone up from his crotch. Adrian couldn't help but look.

'Are you looking at my dick, sir?'

'I'm not looking at your dick, Akker.'

'But you're thinking about my dick. I know you are because I see you looking at me in class. Are you a fag, sir?'

'Akker, my sexuality isn't the issue here.'

'Are you going to hit me then?'

'Jesus Christ, no, I'm not going to hit you. Why would I hit you?'

Akker looked out the side window.

Adrian took two deep breaths and modified his tone. 'Look, I like you – I've always liked you. You're a good kid with plenty of potential. But these stories ...' Adrian didn't know what else to say. He'd somehow lost his resolve.

Akker was still facing the window. 'Do you like the stories, sir?'

Bingo. At least Adrian wasn't going insane, he told himself. 'Sure, to some degree. I mean, they're well written. But I don't know what you're trying to achieve with them. Are you reaching out? Is that what this is?'

Right then the older clerk emerged from a door into the car park, switching on an outdoor light which flooded Adrian's car. The guy put a garbage bag in a wheelie bin and looked over at them. He shut the lid and stood there for a few moments, taking a long look at them. Akker waved two fingers at him, then the guy shut off the light and retreated inside.

'You'd better go,' Adrian said. 'Text your mum.'

Akker picked up his phone and typed. He then slipped the phone into his backpack. 'She'll be here soon. I'll wait out the front.'

'Sure,' Adrian said.

As he drove away, he wondered if he'd accomplished anything that night. The more he thought about it, the more he worried he might only have made matters worse.

*

After that night in the car park nothing exceptional occurred for a month or so. Akker laid low in class. There were no further emails. At lunchtimes Adrian saw him and Marley hanging around together more and more. They put their arms around each other in the way teenage boys do. But one day that all came to an end.

Adrian was on lunch duty when a scuffle broke out, and boys from across the oval ran to the fracas, a mob spurred by mayhem. Adrian rushed over and shouted at them to break it up, break it up. The bell went and the crowd slowly dispersed until just six boys were left, trying to separate two more who were still going at it on the ground. It was more like judo than brawling, but Marley managed to jab his fist into Akker's kidneys several times. At seeing Akker like that, Adrian grabbed Marley by the collar and dragged him aside, tearing his shirt open in the movement. Adrian straightened and looked around, surprised by his own force.

The boys were visibly shocked. 'Fuck! You're hardcore, sir,' one of them said.

'Get to class,' he said. 'All of you. Except you, Marley.'

But Marley grabbed his bag and took off.

Adrian knew he wouldn't get far. 'Go on.'

The audience collected their bags and ambled away, occasionally glancing back.

'Come on, hop up,' Adrian said, putting his hand out to Akker, who accepted it and stood, clutching his side. Adrian helped him to a bench and let him catch his breath.

'What the hell was that all about?'

'Nothing, sir.'

The boy's face was dusty. He had spit across his mouth. His lips were swollen from being rubbed into the pitch.

'Nothing, huh? You don't fight over nothing.'

Akker stood, then looked down at Adrian. 'You should stay out of other people's business.'

'Excuse me?'

'I think you've got problems, sir,' he said, then walked away.

Adrian stayed sitting there for a while, long enough to watch the boy cross the oval and be swallowed by the corridors of the building.

That night another *godhand* email arrived. The third story was attached.

This story was far more explicit – brutal, almost. Something had changed, the ante had been upped. It was structured like a letter, a boy thanking his teacher for what he had shown him – for the lesson in his car that night, when he'd taught him how to fuck a man. How to dominate. How to transform a man into a sissy, with his floppy dick a long, thin clit and his arsehole a cunt. It was unlike anything Adrian had ever read, or desired, and amid the waves of detailed description Adrian realised the depth of the situation. Things were getting out of hand.

He contemplated bringing it to the attention of the school counsellor, but he knew it would get back to Mr H, and he had to avoid that type of intervention. Akker's parents would be called in and a meeting would take place, and Adrian wanted none of that. He knew he'd be questioned as well, and the night in the car park would be discussed and eyebrows raised. Akker had cunningly circled the spotlight onto him, Adrian saw, so he was now implicated in a criminal act. There was a witness – the older clerk – who would confirm Adrian was there that night. Other information could be verified too.

No, none of this can get out, he decided that night. *Surely there's another way. Surely this will end some other way.*

GLENDA

Over the past year, Glenda had intuited a sense of mounting pressure, as though the immunity of the Pomeroy family wouldn't last – that sticks and stones would eventually break their bones. One by one they would be broken, her intuition said. Each family member at a time, beginning with Mal and ending with her. For her suffering was inevitable. Her witnessing of each demise was a knowledge woven into the fabric hanging of the Last Supper on the kitchen wall – not that they'd been religious for a long time.

The Pomeroys had somehow always averted trouble. They'd always proven immune to the misfortunes their neighbours endured, beginning with that month of break-and-enters along their street. Adrian was just six at the time, but at twelve Noel was old enough to comprehend the menace posed to his friends and their families: the mates he hung around with, going over their houses to swim in their pools and play video games or football on the front lawn. When they weren't doing that they were down the creek, building a bush cubby out of scrap timber and tree branches. They'd found convict stone along the creek line and borrowed a wheelbarrow, some tools and Connor's father to shift the rocks, one at a time, as part of their fortifications. Noel had talked about the project a lot for a while, drawing maps of the bush tracks and diagrams of the makeshift architecture. But that all stopped when the break-ins happened.

Half a dozen houses were knocked off over four weeks, including the places on either side of the Pomeroys, plus the one across the street. The Pomeroy house was an island in a stream of thievery. Televisions, VCRs, jewellery and money were the obvious objectives, but some of the houses were graffitied with offensive messages, and fridges were raided and beds urinated on. Noel and Connor and another friend took it upon themselves to be the neighbourhood watch. They dressed in dark clothes, armed themselves with rakes, broomsticks and torches and sat up on the Pomeroy roof for as long as they could. On and off they lasted about a week. And the break-ins had stopped, perhaps because of the boys' vigilance. More likely the crook just moved on. Either way, Glenda believed this was what first motivated Noel to become a police officer.

Noel and his mates didn't return to the cubby for a month or so after that, but when they did they found a mattress inside and plastic bags of clothes and empty food cartons. They talked of the squatter for a while, conjecturing whether it was the burglar, and whether, by extension, they'd aided and abetted him. Glenda called the police and the vagrant cleared out, taking the cubby to pieces before doing so. But after that the trouble in the street only amplified.

First there was a big fire at the housing commission block. It began in one of the ground floor units, where an old man lived. The authorities said he put some chips in the oven late at night and fell asleep in front of the television. Noel said the old guy was dodgy anyway – that he would spot boys riding past on their bikes and ask them inside his unit to show them dirty magazines. The fire made the block structurally unsound, and everyone had to move out until it was repaired.

Then there was the girl found at the creek. Fourteen, and in the grade below Noel at the time. They said she was blindfolded and made to drink from a bottle of vodka until she passed out in the dirt, then the heathen had his way and removed the blindfold and dragged her into the creek to make it look like she'd got drunk and drowned herself. Fingers were pointed at several local boys but no one was charged. Glenda kept a much closer eye on her sons after that, out of fear for their safety. She didn't like to think about the girl, but wondered why she'd been blindfolded if whoever it was had planned on killing her anyway. She put it down to the guilty coward not being able to look his victim in the eye.

During the years the Pomeroys lived in that street, almost everyone was affected by one hardship or another, and amid these events Glenda watched her two sons grow close. At least for a few years. The boys. Her boys.

When she recalled her boys back then, the picture was forever this: the two of them standing side by side, the six years between them measured by inches of height. Noel's arm is draped around his little brother, holding Adrian's shoulder against his hip. Noel owns his blithe smile. Adrian's is more vexed – a sign of his depth of thought and sensitivity, even then. Still, if either child was a cause for concern, Noel was the worry. Not Adrian. Noel's smile hid volatility, a sense of force. Noel was more like his father, who was still dogged in his old-fashioned values: marriage was for a man and a woman only, and tattoos were for criminals. But Mal rarely voiced his beliefs now. Noel was moralistic, staunchly defending the black and white of an issue, whereas Adrian saw the grey. Noel was the risk-taker, the one to jump from a height and walk away; Adrian's hesitation usually meant he'd fall and get hurt. Adrian became a timid boy – not so much weak as reserved, reticent. His introverted nature grated on Noel, who often complained that his little brother was a weirdo because he wouldn't tackle him properly when they played football.

But they did play well together for a time. Noel condescended to playground games, and took Adrian for swims in his friend's pool while the family were on holidays. They often mucked about in the granny flat, reappearing a tad startled whenever she called for them, as though they were so immersed that they'd forgotten about everything else. Boys will be boys, Glenda conceded, but she liked to think she had a solid clutch on what her sons got up to, and that her trust was central in defining their relationship with her. The long lead she afforded them meant they were less likely to take advantage of that trust.

Glenda also liked to think that although the Pomeroys were never a well-to-do family, what they lacked in wealth they made up for in love.

★

But now this – this feeling of an end drawing ever closer, heralded by the young upstart at the medical centre ten months ago. Despite the doctor's wariness to diagnose, she knew he was right. She knew this better than anyone because she was the closest witness to – and common casualty of – her husband's changed behaviour. *Victim* was too strong a word, but he had become something to endure.

That day, in the vapid waiting room at the medical centre in Merrylands, she put a car magazine on Mal's lap and told him to stay while she renewed her prescription. But in truth what she needed was an ally.

The doctor was a young man, there in place of their regular doctor, who was on leave for a few months. She was hesitant to tell him at first — she never had anyone to complain to about her husband's drinking so she wasn't in the habit — but the young doctor had a gentle way about him and he coaxed the story from her. It helped that he reminded her of Adrian, although darker-skinned. An utter professional, yet empathetic. She knew this from his hands and his voice.

So she told him everything that had been going on. About how Mal had begun repeating himself, only occasionally at first but almost constantly now, and how he forgot things he'd done. That he found it difficult to plan ahead. That he was hard to motivate — the half-complete kit car beneath a sheet of tarpaulin behind the garage was testament to that. He'd been building the car since the boys were young. The prospect of not completing it had once been an agony for Mal, but lately he'd become apathetic about it, as about most things, and he'd let the grass grow high around it. And sometimes it was like he forgot who people were and what things were called, so she had to remind him.

Glenda worried that the doctor might say these were just symptoms of ageing, that he wouldn't perceive the gravity of it. 'My husband is no longer my husband,' she said tearfully. The doctor didn't make her explain any further — he seemed to understand. He asked about the possible causes, the specific effects. She said it happened not just when Mal was drinking, and the doctor asked how many units of alcohol he normally consumed each week. She didn't know. 'He makes his own grappa,' she said, 'and he gets through several bottles – four, five.' She never really counted.

'I think it's best you bring him in,' the doctor said. 'I'll need to talk to him before making a diagnosis.'

Glenda thought of Mal's garage, which was often the subject of neighbourly talk. He liked to keep stuff, especially mechanical or electrical things which might still be of some use, even if damaged. Old televisions, radios, cooking appliances and other mechanisms Glenda could not name. He kept these things and his tools and auto parts on shelves, and at the back of the garage he brewed his grappa in large plastic drums. She loathed the *blip, blip, blip* those drums made. She could hear them in the house. Sometimes she heard them at night, in bed.

'Some days I don't think I can take any more,' she said.

The doctor nodded. 'I understand. I need to see your husband, talk to him, make some observations to get a clearer understanding of what we are dealing with.'

'He'll tell you what he thinks is true,' she said. 'With the drinking especially. And beyond that he doesn't know what he's like because he doesn't remember any of it.'

More sympathetic nodding. 'Okay,' he said. 'Just from what you've said it sounds similar to alcohol-related dementia – the symptoms are consistent with other forms of dementia so it can be difficult to diagnose. Considering your husband's long-term alcohol consumption, there's a chance he has some frontal lobe damage. Some practitioners refer to it as wet brain. But again—'

'Like he's pickled his brain?'

'You could put it that way. Yes. But again, I must see him to make a diagnosis.'

That was when Glenda began to slip. She felt herself diminish into the chair. As though it had swallowed some internal part of her. 'Can he get better?'

'Depending on how the consultation goes, if ARD seems to be what you're dealing with, then I'll refer him to a specialist.'

'But is it reversible?'

'That depends.'

'On what?'

He said what she knew he would say: there was a chance he could recover some of his former brain and physiological function, but it depended on the extent of his alcohol consumption, and he would have to abstain. Glenda knew her husband. Forty-three years of marriage assured that knowledge.

She may have said something about understanding: she couldn't recall. She could only remember looking at the photo frame on his desk – with a boy and a girl and a pretty woman. It was taken in a playground. She could see part of a slide in the background on one edge of the photo, and monkey bars on the other. For some reason this calmed her; the knowledge that the young doctor was a parent, that he knew what it was to have that joyful yet grave sense of responsibility, made her feel okay.

'I'll bring him in,' she said, then she stood and closed the door behind her and went back to the waiting room. Daytime television was showing in the corner, the volume low, with old people and a mother with a murmuring baby sitting in the three rows of beige plastic chairs.

Mal was still there, at the end of the first row. He looked up at her with the eyes of a sad dog, the magazine open in his lap. 'Done?' he said.

Over the years she had learned to take her husband with a pinch of salt. The man who once brought her down with as little as a good hard stare was now the family labrador. And a labrador who chased his own tail at that.

'Yes,' she said, lifting her handbag to her shoulder. 'All done.'

★

Now Glenda found herself reaching into the recycling bin. She knew he wouldn't have thrown the brochure away on purpose – he'd never complained about the tickets so she was sure it was just his memory loss. Grappa was just finding new ways to affect their lives. And this one would be her house, no one else's – they could and would try, of course, but this time it was her time, her luck, because luck is when opportunity meets preparation and Glenda was certainly well prepared. In fact, she'd been priming her luck over the past ten months, making it into something of a hobby. Mal had his grappa, she had her charity prize homes.

At sixty-two, Glenda had given up on buying her own home. It was one of those commitments they had never managed to achieve, because by the time they gained a sense of financial security they were quite beyond entering the pricey Sydney market. They'd lived in the Merrylands rental for a very long time now, after downsizing when Adrian left for university. The owner allowed them to treat it as theirs: small renovation projects were fine. Friends who visited assumed they owned it, perhaps because the house had become an extension of them.

The neighbours joked that Mal and Glenda were permanently

preparing for a jumble sale that would never happen. *Jumbled* was one word, *cluttered* was another; Glenda preferred *eclectic*. Mal had his garage but Glenda had her own paraphernalia. After retiring from nursing with a disability pension due to her terrible back, she took up crocheting patchwork blankets for the local animal shelter, and had collected elephant figurines ever since a friend from the shelter brought one back as a gift from Kenya. After then, people gave her elephants if they didn't know what else to get. It was a collection grown by convenience rather than choice.

Ever since that day at the medical centre, she'd been feathering a new vision for her future, one without Mal, and winning a lottery house was a significant part of that vision.

She received the brochures in the mail, but she also used the internet to take virtual tours of these houses. She especially liked the furnishings – picture frames with the kinds of artworks she'd never choose for her walls at home. She couldn't help feeling a strange attraction to somebody else's taste. And the fact that these houses could be hers, with a handful of tickets and some luck, was the ultimate draw. Yet at heart it was less about her than about her children and grandchildren. People often asked what she would do with the house if she won, but it didn't really matter if she sold it or moved into it because the outcome would be the same: she would live with Adrian and his family in her old age, helping out with meals and looking after Tam and any other little ones they might be blessed with. God willing. Whether that life was in a prize home or a home purchased with money from its sale was unimportant.

Glenda retrieved the brochure from the bin, then went inside to put the kettle on. Through the kitchen window she could see Mal at the back table, sipping grappa, doing sudoku. She filled the kettle, depressed the power button and was unfolding the brochure on the kitchen benchtop when the doorbell rang. 'Are you expecting anyone?' she called to Mal, out of habit. He shook his head.

The bell chimed again as Glenda walked towards it. Her intuition felt active again, her internal barometer indicating that change waited on the other side of the door. Through the glass she saw the figures of Tam and Nguyet, suitcases in hand.

THREE

THREE

ADRIAN

The cops dropped Adrian home in a police vehicle. He wasn't cuffed, but that wouldn't have made any difference. The damage was already written.

He had to knock on the front door because he was without keys. Noo answered. Beside her, in the doorway, was a suitcase. In the lounge room he could hear Tam playing a video game – the *ping* and *kapow* of stylised barbarism.

'You said you'd wait it out with me,' Adrian told her. No hello. She was clearly confused.

'Yesterday at the hospital. You said you'd wait it out.'

Noo was incredulous now. Of course she only meant she'd wait at the hospital. She hadn't known, then, about all this. She'd had to get the female officer to explain as he was put into the back of the police vehicle. She'd had to lie to Tam. This is what she told Adrian as she picked up the suitcase and walked it out to the boot of the car.

'Can't I at least defend myself? In my words?'

But she wasn't to be stopped. She called out to Tam, who reluctantly turned off the console. He came outside and put an arm around his dad's leg, then got into the car. The engine kicked over and Noo reversed out of the driveway. She pulled up alongside the concrete path and wound down the window. Adrian walked over, hopeful, but she'd only stopped to tell him about the note.

'What note?'

The note she found nailed to the door when she came home from the school run, after the police had finished going through the house, his study, taking things away. She'd put it in the kitchen, in an envelope.

Adrian nodded but his heart cleaved. From the back seat Tam waved his little hand, cheerfully, none the wiser. At least Adrian could feel grateful for that.

Inside, he found the note on the cutting board. It was handwritten. Crudely. But the characteristics of the writing belied the force that six words could create.

I'm coming for you sick fuck.

Adrian folded the note back into the envelope, then tore the whole thing up and put the pieces in the bin. He pulled a bottle of wine from the cupboard and poured a glass, drank it rapidly. He went to pour another but decided on his dad's home-made grappa instead. He didn't like it much but taste held no meaning at that moment. He poured, drank, poured another.

He sat at the dining table and stared at the bin in the corner of the kitchen.

You're not thinking right, he realised. *You shouldn't have done that. You should keep it.*

Then Bowman's face came to mind and the name finally occurred to him: Danny. Danny Bowman. The recognition stirred Adrian to get up, retrieve the note and get a roll of sticky tape. He downed his grappa and poured another, and sat at the table to piece the note together. When he had finished he found a new envelope and put the note inside, sealed it and placed it in a desk drawer in his study. He could report it but he didn't want the cops on his doorstep yet again. He'd keep it for the trial – if it came to that.

His study had been ransacked. The police had been orderly enough – there weren't papers all over the floor and drawers upturned. They'd left neat piles of inconsequentials: the documentation they could access electronically, folders of curriculum papers, receipts, a stack of Tam's drawings, other bits and pieces. But they'd taken what he had suspected they'd target. And although he'd resigned himself to this fact, he couldn't help feeling violated, staring at the gap on his desk where the computer normally sat. He thought about the emails from Akker and those stories and his guts roiled.

He closed the door and went back to the kitchen. Over more grappa he wondered why he wasn't that upset about Nguyet, or worried – but there were few places she could go, and the mostly likely was his mother's. Glenda would always welcome Noo and Tam with open arms, regardless of their awkward cultural differences, like Noo's refusal to cheek-kiss, and Mal's doubt about Adrian's choice of wife. His father had never said anything, but words weren't necessary.

Mal had been at the back table doing sudoku the day Adrian told his mother about the Vietnamese girl he'd met on the internet; he realised Mal had been listening when the old man's laughter burst through the kitchen curtain. Adrian knew the words 'mail-order bride' had been on repeat in his father's head ever since. It wasn't long after that Adrian left for Vietnam during the term break, to discover whether their relationship would be as promising in person as online. They'd been Skyping for almost a year by then, so it wasn't impulsive. Adrian had known there was a good chance he would return married, but he didn't tell his mother that before he left. He couldn't recall ever lying to her during his adult life, but there was a difference between lying and not volunteering information. She simply had to ask the right questions. She rarely asked the truly hard ones.

They held an unofficial wedding ceremony when Nguyet arrived in Australia several months later. A modest celebration, with a mock exchange of rings and iteration of vows. But a slight shake of the head during the ceremony was all it took to make Mal's impressions clear. Adrian didn't know why he'd even looked at his father at that moment, but it occurred to him that perhaps, in some masochistic corner of his heart, he desired his father's approval. How predictable. How sad. Especially considering that when he'd first introduced Nguyet to his family, Mal had joked about her being flat-chested and wondered if she was 'one of them Asian girly-boys'. He couldn't pronounce her name easily so he persisted in calling her 'Lim' when she was around, or 'Lim the Shim' when she wasn't. Adrian always pulled him up on that but to no effect. Tam's arrival didn't change much. The boy's name was a source of confusion for Mal, who, when it was announced, gave nothing more than a derisive 'rightio'.

Yep, they'd be with Glenda and Mal now, suffering the indignities of his father's racism, his mum getting cross, telling him to stop it. She was an accepting woman when it came to most things, and Adrian often sensed her empathy when it came to Mal's brusqueness. She too knew what it was to endure him.

Adrian put the glass on the kitchen sink and turned on the light. It was evening now and he knew he had to make the call. The thought crossed his mind that the home phone might be tapped, but he wondered if that was just something that happened on television shows to increase the drama. It didn't matter, though, because calling Glenda was no longer a choice. There was a decent chance she already knew.

He picked up the phone and dialled the number he knew so well. When he heard the dial tone, he realised he was hoping that Noo had already done his dirty work.

'Mum.'

'Hello, darling.'

'Is she there?'

'They're both here. They're fine. And they can stay for as long as needed.'

'Okay, but hopefully it won't be for long.' He tried not to slur his words. The grappa was taking hold.

'I don't know why she's chosen to do this right now, though,' Glenda said. 'Surely you need her support.'

'So she told you.'

'Well, I suppose so.'

'About the accident.'

'Yes.'

He heard an intake of breath. He knew this feeling. This breathing it through.

'And the rest of it,' she said.

And now he was the one breathing it through. Just like when he was a teenager, confessing to her something wholly humiliating. And yet this was far grimmer than admitting to his first drink or trying weed.

'I'm sorry,' he said, though he didn't know whether he was apologising for not being the one to tell her or for something harder to think about. Perhaps it was for everything – for all the things he'd never shared with her, the things he knew would rock her to the point of … if not heart attack, then at the very least a heartache so great it would dismantle her understanding of her family and the disgrace they had succumbed to.

'It's okay,' she said. 'It doesn't matter who told me.'

Guilt.

'It's my fault you found out that way.'

Then she referred to him by name and said that she loved him. This, he knew, was the beginning of her undoing.

'But I've got so many things wrong,' he said. 'I should've handled it all some other way.' He thought of Fielder's questions.

'What's the school doing about it?'

Zilch. 'They're doing what they have to,' he said.

'Are they on your side?'

'I'm sure they're trying to keep a lid on it.'

'But who's on your side?'

He should've asked himself that already. Now Adrian realised he needed to talk to someone from the school – someone on staff with an ear for student chatter. He thought of a couple of people.

'I don't know. I haven't been home all that long, and the police took my mobile and computer. I'll make some calls, though.'

'So you're not still teaching?'

'I'm suspended with pay until the police sort it out.'

'And what did the police say?'

'There isn't enough evidence to charge me yet. But they said not to go anywhere.' He considered making a joke about bussing it to Queensland.

'We can lend you a car. Not to leave, of course. Just to get around.'

His mother knew him better than he knew himself sometimes. 'It's okay. I'll be fine.'

'Don't be ridiculous.'

'But …' Here was the hardest question of all. 'What are you going to tell Dad?'

Again, her intake of breath. Adrian held his.

'I'll tell him the truth. I'll tell him that you've had an accident and you need to borrow our car. There's nothing else to say at the moment. You're not guilty, are you?'

★

Adrian was severely fatigued and drunk and wondered how he would continue to manage the run of emotion, but he needed to talk to someone from school. He thought of Witmer. As head of English, Witmer would be across it all. He had the personality to see through the politics, to know the black from the white. Some savvy student had nicknamed him Mr Meek, and while it wasn't unjustified, he was also adept at strategy. He was a mover – people just didn't suspect it. Adrian could count on him for some inside knowledge.

He picked up the phone, dialled.

'Witmer.'

'Adrian?'

'Yeah, look, I was hoping we—'

'I'm sorry, Adrian, but I'm not comfortable talking to you right now.'

'Can I call back?' He knew his was the voice of a desperate man, but he didn't care.

'No, you don't understand. I'm not comfortable talking to you at all. This is wrong. What you did to that boy is wrong.'

Adrian tried to think of some meaningful rebuttal. He had nothing.

'I'm sorry,' Witmer said, but Adrian was already hanging up.

Next he tried Rafiq. Rafiq was a good friend. Sometimes the two of them played squash on Thursday nights, and he and his wife had come around for dinner twice. They were decent people, progressive. Amy was a new Muslim. They had two boys, eight and six. If he couldn't count on Rafiq, then he couldn't count on anyone.

He dialled the number. It rang out. He tried again, and this time the ringing cut short, like the phone was abruptly switched off. Like what someone does when they're rejecting a call.

Adrian put the phone down and rubbed at the wadding on his nose. He peeled the bandage off, looked at the gauze and placed it blood-side-up on the edge of the kitchen sink. He put a fingertip to the laceration and pulled it away to see fresh blood. He'd removed the bandage too early and torn some of the clotted blood away. He had to be more patient. This wasn't going to be resolved so quickly.

'Control yourself,' he said aloud.

He then picked up the glass from the sink and pitched it against the wall.

★

He lives only a ten- or fifteen-minute drive from the old house. He sometimes imagines going back there to have a poke around, to see what recollections still haunt the place. The good ghosts, the not-so-good ghosts. He wonders what he would discover there, though. The bricks and fibrocement are still in place – he knows this, has seen this from a distance, the startled face still there, its eyes wide open – but Adrian has come so far since then that the memories have become stretched. He feels the tension in them – the fraying of smell and sound and touch and taste. The visions are the strongest yet time has uncoiled them as well. These memories, they are fraught.

Yet there are certain knowledges etched in his physiognomy. His skin might renew itself every few weeks but that does not alter its grain, and the imprint it leaves. He knows things, even while he does not know how he knows them. And this was always his difficulty: by the time he came to realise what had gone on, what he had done with his own hands and lips and fingertips and tongue, five or six years had passed. It was a revelation that arrived with puberty.

Since then, he has wondered if there is some science behind this, a connection between pubertal growth and the tapping of stored information – via new synapses perhaps, linking the effects of the past, the unfamiliar sensations felt by a young body, to the developing logic of a twelve-year-old. But then again, a muscle doesn't have to know that it's made of tissue and blood vessels, tendons and nerves in order to flex. It just is and does. And that is precisely how those memories came to inscribe themselves on Adrian Pomeroy. Like writing on his skull. Like words his blood flows over, but still he cannot read and thereby know. Not for sure.

If only a word of truth could be uttered, by someone.

★

Adrian let himself slip with remarkable haste that first night alone.

He sat on the front steps and drank more grappa and half a bottle of wine, watching the street go about its business. City workers pulling into driveways. Shoppers. Night-time dog walkers. A kid with a backpack, probably coming home from a mate's place. Thoughts of these other people and their homely lives distracted him from his own sudden loss of normality – but only for a short while. Despair had wormed its way into the meat of him and the booze only emphasised its bite. He resisted any urge to cry, though, because his anguish was seeding anger, not surrender.

Yet this antagonism was not for a particular person. Not Akker, not Fielder, not Noo for leaving, not even himself for breathing life into this zombie-like scenario – he almost laughed at the realisation that he had become the walking dead. No, this anger was less defined, more liberal, in both senses of the word. His seething was a nondescript, dormant energy; almost an apathetic hatred of the fact that these circumstances had become him.

All there was left to do was drink and pop a couple of 5-milligram diazepam tablets, prescribed by his dentist. 'You'll crack a tooth one day,' the guy had said; Adrian was grinding so hard in his sleep that grooves were worn into the enamel. 'Something stressing you lately?'

What a question ... And what a fucking answer.

ALEX

Michaela and Danny separated in the summer after Year Seven, and thoughts of Mr Pomeroy drifted to the back of Alex's mind.

The separation brought him both relief and confusion. Michaela didn't cry when she kicked Danny out, and Alex knew why. Her mum had visited the day before, while Danny was at his cleaning job, and they'd sat and talked. They talked through the afternoon and into the evening, keeping Alex and Shannon out of the room, though the two sat in the hallway from time to time, listening, the women only pausing to give the kids some dinner.

Michaela's mother called a spade a spade. 'Danny's just not a very nice person,' she told Michaela. 'He's got you in a rut. Divorce might be a hard road to take, but you can't keep hurting like this. You've got to do something about it.'

Although Alex didn't fully understand what that hurt was, he'd seen the stress in his mum's face enough to know that she wasn't happy. Hadn't been for a long time, he figured, and that night he saw her cry so much there at the kitchen bench that he felt like crying as well. And so by the time Alex witnessed his parents' separation the following day, Michaela had no more tears left.

She waited until Danny woke from his overnight shift. She made him bacon and baked beans, waited till he was finished, then sat him on their bed and took his hands. Shannon was at a neighbour's house; Alex watched from the lounge room.

'Danny, listen, I've been thinking about us and the kids heaps lately, and—'

'Yeah, what?'

'And I've been feeling a certain way for a long time, and I don't think it's good that I feel this way.'

'What? Piss off.'

'I'm serious, Danny. Listen to me, I don't—'

'Don't start this shit again. It's all good. Money gets a bit tight sometimes, but it's—'

'No, it's not all good, and that's my point. You're working two jobs and I'm getting these bookkeeping jobs coming through, and we never get to see each other, and when we do you're always getting on the piss or sleeping or yelling at the kids, and then we argue about it.'

'Bullshit. We haven't argued for ages.'

'That's only because I've been holding back, or because you're not here to argue with.'

'That's because I'm working hard – hard for you! So what if I have a few drinks, have a yell? You're alright. I don't hit you or anything.'

'I want something different from—'

'From what, me working my arse off for you and the kids?'

'Yes, exactly. I want something different for the kids, for us. For you, most of all.'

'Right, and for yourself by the sounds of it.'

'Exactly. I'm not happy living like this. Something has to change or I'll go fucking mental. So I want you to leave. For a while. Just see what happens,' she said, and Danny said nothing.

Alex held his breath, waiting for his old man to rage, to break shit, to smash a hole in the wall again, to punch the framed photograph of the family who no longer wanted him. But he did none of those things. He got up from the bed, put clothes and shoes in a bag, and refused to look at his wife, quaking as though the surface of his heart had split. Shannon came home while he packed and Alex told her what was happening. She said nothing.

Their father grabbed his wallet and keys and phone from the kitchen and headed towards the door. Then he did something Alex wasn't expecting – he came up and kissed both his kids on the head.

'She can kick me out of the house, but you're still my kids, okay? I'll be around,' he told them.

*

Danny moved into a flat not far from his family's home and continued to pay for some of the bills. The kids didn't visit his flat on a regular basis but Michaela said he could come back home on the weekends, so he ate dinner with them every Saturday.

Over the next year, without his father around much, Alex started to take on more responsibility. With this emergent sense of importance, he found it easier to ignore, most of the time, those feelings he'd had for Mr Pomeroy, putting them in their place by reasoning that it was probably just his hormones. He had a different English teacher, so he only saw Mr Pomeroy at assembly or in the yard at lunchtime, and whenever he got that pang again, that compulsion, that sense of a developing need, he tried to distract himself with his mates or schoolwork or whatever was going on at home. He also tried to remember shame.

By the time Alex was sixteen he'd become a young man, and with this came a new sense of self. No longer the boy in need of a believer, he was coming to understand his own potency. No longer would his dad raise a belt to him – instead, he would raise his own hand to the world.

'Look at you, ay?' his father said at dinner one Saturday. 'Finally got some hair on that upper lip, like a real man.' Danny grabbed his forearm and shook it hard.

'That actually hurts,' Alex said.

Danny laughed. 'But not a man yet!'

Shannon looked at her father. 'What about me, Dad?'

'Yeah, you're lookin' more and more like your mum,' he said, then put a forkful of rice in his mouth and spoke through it, though the words struck nevertheless. 'But that doesn't mean you've got an excuse for making the same mistakes she has.'

Alex didn't know which of her decisions his dad was referring to: the separation, or falling for him in the first place.

Later that night, after Danny left for his flat and Alex was in his bedroom, his mum came to him and put her hands on his shoulders. 'Don't think you have to be the man he is, okay? You can be your own man. Who loves others in the ways he wants to love them.'

'I know,' he said.

She kissed his forehead and gave him some space.

On the first day of Year Eleven, not long after that Saturday night, Mr Pomeroy walked into the classroom and Alex's heart swelled in a way he had to fight with new resolve. The habit of denial had become so entrenched by then that at first his feelings hit him with genuine surprise. He'd grown into his adolescent body, put on some muscle bulk, but he had also grown a new mindset. He'd hardened up. He'd learned how to sit back in his seat and put on an air of not knowing much and not really caring. And he now had mates who called him Akker, and he wore this name as a badge of their camaraderie.

It was for this reason, he told himself, that he approached Mr Pomeroy's desk at the end of that first English class of the year. To show just how much he'd changed.

'What's up, Alex?'

Mr Pomeroy was tidying the lesson's paperwork on his desk. Akker liked watching him being busy.

'I'd like to be called Akker in class, sir.'

'Sure, Akker. Not a problem. It's good to have you in my classroom again,' Mr Pomeroy said, to which Akker felt a surge of what he thought had been neatly buried. He was so unnerved that a smirk broke across his mouth.

'I look forward to being nurtured, sir,' he said. He couldn't help the tease, even though it was only drawing out that buried thing. It was as though some part of him desired to begin something new from something old.

That night, in bed, he reflected on the many things that had happened over the past four years, plus all that hadn't happened. Although he was transformed on the surface, the one element of himself he'd done so well to conceal had, after all this time, not altered at all. And he knew – he could see it in Mr Pomeroy's eyes, in the subtleties of his body language – that there was reciprocal feeling. A spark. A burn. He could see heat there in Mr Pomeroy's expression.

That night, Alex finally gave in to the thought of Adrian Pomeroy – and not Adrian Pomeroy the teacher, but Adrian Pomeroy the man.

*

Getting to Adrian's house was a little difficult the first time, but after that Akker knew the way and even memorised the bus route. Finding out his address online wasn't all that complicated.

There was risk, for sure, that he'd get caught and have to explain what the hell he was doing stalking his teacher. The only possible justifications he could come up with involved turning the tables, deflecting the accusations, making Adrian into something he wasn't. Then again, it wasn't as if Adrian was exactly rejecting the attention – mostly just looks in class, at that point. He seemed to like it.

But there was no chance Akker would tell the truth because that would mean more shame than he could bear. And anyway, he wasn't quite sure what the truth of the situation was. Can impressions and thoughts be told as some definitive truth? He reckoned not.

So he strategised, telling his mum he'd been called in for an evening work shift. He'd ask her to drop him off at the store, and from there bus it across suburbs and walk the remaining few blocks to the house. By the time he arrived it was always dark enough to slip up the driveway and along the side of the house, where he could move from window to window, watching Adrian go about his night. There was a perverse pleasure in seeing this other side to his teacher, his domestic qualities. He'd watch him play with his son on the floor or read books together or watch TV. Seeing the way Adrian interacted with his family didn't put Akker off at all. It brought a sense of intimacy that he couldn't get in the classroom. It was a kind of privilege to witness the real Adrian, the man beyond the teacher at the front of the room, and Akker's feelings strengthened.

Not even seeing Adrian's wife deterred him. If anything, knowing who she was dispelled the woman of his imagination, who was far more incredible than the reality. He was relieved at her ordinariness – her looks, her backgrounded presence in the house. He was also relieved by the lack of affection she showed Adrian. They hardly touched, let alone did anything more sexual. From the outside, they looked like a couple on the verge of slipping away from one another, urged by the invisible force of diminishing love. He never caught them arguing or witnessed a decisive action, but Akker had seen enough to know that such a marriage couldn't last. And although he wanted it that way, sometimes he wished he could reach in through the window and hold them both. At other times, he desired to take Adrian away from the hurt he could not see coming.

Over eight visits spanning a few months, Akker never saw Adrian naked, but on a few nights he saw him in his underwear or with a towel around his waist, and this turned him on even more. Especially when he imagined what he would find once that towel was peeled away. Sometimes he convinced himself that Adrian knew he was being watched, and that he was putting on a kind of show – a display of his masculinity, a demonstration of the love he was capable of giving.

When Adrian showed up at the store one night, Akker took it as a sign. When his shift ended he went home, and there wrote the first story he'd created for Adrian since he was twelve. Two days later he opened an email account under the name *godhand*. Using this account, he sent Adrian the story. It was meant to be a love story. A gesture of touch. The story was meant to portray Adrian as his saviour.

★

Adrian's behaviour changed after that first email. He never said anything, never mentioned what he thought of the story or even acknowledged receiving it, but Akker knew his teacher was watching him more closely. Whenever doubt surfaced – that perhaps he shouldn't have emailed under an alias – Akker found reassurance in a glance, a turning of the lip, or the emphasis Adrian put on a word when he read aloud from the Golding book they were studying in class.

Then came the day in the library.

Akker had an assignment to complete for ancient history so he went to find reference materials during his free period. He walked the shelves and found what he needed, then carried the pile to the quiet study zone, a room towards the rear of the building where there were beanbags and armchairs. When he entered he looked up to see Adrian lounging in one of the armchairs, reading a novel. No one else was around.

Akker watched him and sat in one of the chairs nearby. Adrian didn't seem to notice him at first, so Akker opened a book and flipped through pages, looking up every few seconds. Adrian read, moving his lips mutely as he did so, as if he were in a trance.

Then the trance broke. He looked up. They made eye contact.

'Sir.'

'Mr Bowman,' Adrian said. The teacher tried to go back to his book, but failed. He dropped it to his lap. 'Why are you in here, Akker? Shouldn't you be in class?'

Akker felt his heart sucking blood from his body's extremities. 'Free period, sir. Doing some research for an assignment.'

'Right. And I just happen to be sitting here.'

Akker looked around, then back at his teacher. 'A coincidence,' Adrian said.

'Yeah, I guess so.'

'Right.'

Akker didn't appreciate Adrian's expression; it was like he was taking the piss or something. 'What book are you reading, sir?'

'This.' Adrian held up the hardback copy of *The Stories of John Cheever*. 'I just picked it up off the shelf.'

'Sure. Any good?'

'A bit heavy, you could say.'

Akker nodded.

'It can be difficult to find a storyteller you like,' Adrian continued.

'Yeah. Stories are good.'

'Stories are important because they allow us to make sense of our lives,' Adrian said, playing the teacher's role more faithfully now.

'Yeah, but they're better than life because we can be who we want in them.'

Adrian nodded. He turned a page.

Akker smirked, and they both returned to their books. They could've been just two people reading.

When the bell rang Adrian closed his book, then came over to Akker and stood behind his chair. He reached out and put his hand on Akker's shoulder, leaving it there a moment, looking down at the book Akker held, perhaps at the very same words he was reading. Adrian seemed reluctant to pull away. Perhaps, Akker wondered, out of lust. Or perhaps because removing the hand would draw more attention to it.

'Can't we stay?' Akker asked.

'No,' Adrian said. 'We can't.'

Then Adrian took his hand back and walked away.

But Akker didn't move. Akker didn't move for a very long time.

★

Late that Saturday night, Akker wrote the second story as a dedication to what was unsaid. There was risk in telling this story, because there was a good chance Adrian would realise Akker had been to his house at some point – the evidence was there in the description. If Adrian responded with anger, he decided, he would deny it. Denial was the easiest card to play. After all, he'd played it many times before – he had done so that very evening, when his dad spoke to him after dinner.

Michaela had stood and begun taking the plates from the table. Danny looked to Shannon. 'Go give your mother a hand in the kitchen.' Shannon did as she was asked.

'Alex, you didn't finish your dinner,' Danny began. 'What's up, mate?'

He shook his head. 'Not hungry.'

'You know I hate it when you kids waste food.'

'Not hungry, I said.' He put his elbows on the table and sank his head into his palms.

Years ago, his old man would've threatened to get the belt

out for that kind of behaviour, but so much had changed. Maybe now he feared the return of his son's hand.

Danny moved his chair closer and bent towards Akker's face. 'Mate, I've been watching you for a couple of weeks. Is there something going on I should know about?'

'It's nothing, Dad.'

'Well, I reckon there's at least something.' Danny tried to pull Akker's hand from his face. 'Look at me when I'm speaking to you.'

Akker didn't budge.

'What about school – you keeping up with tests and all that?'

'Yep.'

'Your mates giving you trouble?'

'No.'

'What about your teachers?'

'No, Dad.' Akker lifted his head now and rocked back in his chair.

'What about work? Is that manager giving you shit shifts still? Mum says you've been working more lately. Just don't throw away this chance you've got at school, okay? Don't be a dickhead like me, right? School's more important than money at the moment. And we didn't—'

'I know, Dad. And I've got nothing to say to you. I'm in control.'

Danny sat back in his chair. 'Well. I hope you are.'

ADRIAN

Adrian woke to Glenda tapping on his bedroom window with a key. He could make out her shape through the slicing blinds and her voice through muffling glass. He didn't move and she didn't tap long. He heard her walk around to the front of the house, and guessed she left the key under the mat or somewhere not too conspicuous. He heard the sound of his dad's ute start up and pull away, then he got up and yanked the blind cord down and the room got dark enough that he could go back to sleep.

He woke again late morning. He fixed himself a coffee and was sweeping the shards of glass from the kitchen benchtop and floor onto some newspaper when the phone rang.

'Is this Adrian?'

'Rafiq?'

'Yeah, you caught me at a bad time yesterday but I'm glad you called.'

'Look, I just need to talk to someone about what's going on.'

'I bet you do. There's been a bit of talk at school you should probably know about. I have a class soon and I don't want to talk about it like this, but could you meet at the squash courts at five o'clock?'

Adrian looked out at his mother's car, delivered to his driveway. 'Sure.'

*

As he drove, he tried to recall the dream he'd been having before he woke. Adrian almost always remembered his dreams for a while, before leaving them behind. Even the ones about banal acts and everyday emotions – the kind which failed to leave their mark on the day they precede. The sieved stuff of ordinariness. It seemed that those forgettable dreams were only important to be had, rather than remembered. Dreams to get things clear, for thoughts from the day to arrange themselves, to find a place somewhere in the box that was his brain.

But then there were the dreams he knew must form a map of him. The kind which recurred or reached for some truth, if only he could pull back and take a good look at what they revealed beyond their abstract quality. These were the kinds of dreams that left an impression on his skin, in his muscle, like the sweat and ache of physical exertion.

This morning's dream was so vivid that it felt like a real event. Two boys, one older, one younger, both with equally dark heads, wrestling on a bed. The older boy laughed at his own strength as the younger tried to tackle him into the covers, but the older boy only had to manoeuvre himself over the top of his brother to pin him against the bed, using his size and weight. He then pulled the covers over his brother and held the end down. The young one screamed a muffled cry to let him out but the older boy laughed again, believing that he knew the limits, the point of suffocation, and that his brother would be fine if he let him go in time.

The screaming became more frantic. He kicked beneath the covers. He cried. He let out a gurgling sound and finally his brother let the cover go.

The young one kicked out again and his heel collided with his brother, knocking him to the floor, but he was laughing still. This sent the younger boy into a rage, his face wet with crying and saliva. He got up from the bed and picked up a heavy book from the shelf, then while his brother had his face turned the young boy brought the book down on the back of the dark head. The head bent forward awkwardly, the body rocking, so the young boy took advantage and hit him again and again, and then once more, until Adrian woke with the tangibility of impact.

★

'Salaam, my brother.' Rafiq shook Adrian's hand, placing his left hand over their clasped hands.

'And peace be with you.'

'Oh, I think you are in greater need at present.' He was looking at the patch over Adrian's nose. 'How are you holding up? You don't look like the Adrian I know.'

'I guess I'm doing as well as can be expected. It feels like the drama's only just begun.'

'Well, I'm pleased you've come. It must be difficult, and I have some things to tell you.'

'The hit-out will be good anyway. Clear my head a little.'

They picked up their racquets and Rafiq opened the glass door to a court.

'So what's this news?' Adrian said. 'I'll serve first.'

'Well, you know these boys. There's only black and white for them. They tease each other, taunt each other. There's a very thin line between friend and foe.'

Adrian served as he listened. He gave the ball too much and he faulted.

'There's certainly no grey for many of them,' Adrian said, and served again.

Rafiq returned and the point was over quickly. He took up the serve. 'They're still making sense of the world. And where they are placed within it.'

Rafiq's blend of faith, tolerance and intelligence was what made him such a good teacher. Adrian appreciated that more than ever now. He felt as though he had become Rafiq's student in that moment.

'Maybe a few months ago I had a Year Eleven class in the change rooms, and I was outside marking the roll when I overheard some talk. They were teasing each other, saying things about being gay, then someone mentioned Akker. Akker's the faggot, they said.'

When Adrian heard those words put together that way, echoing off the squash court walls, he missed a shot. He kicked the ball back to Rafiq.

Rafiq continued. 'Do you remember the fight between Akker and Marley on the oval? They say it was because Akker touched him in the shower – touched his genitals, you know – and Akker was hard.'

There was no need for Rafiq to say anything further. If the boys at school doubted Akker's sexuality, then the peer pressure, the goading, the sledging would probably be enough to push him to deflect guilt elsewhere. Adrian dropped his racquet on the floor and knelt.

Rafiq squatted beside him. 'Are you okay?'

'I'm fine. It's just ... It doesn't explain everything, but it explains enough.'

'I don't believe Alex Bowman is a bad person. Neither is his English teacher.'

Adrian nodded.

'Tell me, how is Nguyet taking it?'

'I don't really know. It doesn't look like happy days, though – she's taken Tam to stay with my parents.'

'This makes sense. There is a saying: when things are too hard to handle, retreat and count your blessings. She needs time and space. Give her your respect and faith and she will return. Amy would need the same if such a thing happened to me.'

'But it wouldn't happen to you. That's the thing – it wouldn't happen to a guy like you.'

They both stood and Adrian picked up his racquet. Rafiq served and Adrian returned once, but then lost the will to continue. He let the ball bounce in his square and roll to a stop against the glass.

Rafiq turned to him. 'You will find peace in the truth of this situation. That truth may be a burning coal you must hold, but you will live and you will know it.'

★

The next afternoon, Danny Bowman was back outside the house in his grey Camry, no doubt still burning for revenge. Retaliation. Retribution. Exacted upon those parts of Adrian's body which had disgraced his son, beginning with his eyes for looking at the boy, then his hands for putting them on the boy, and finally his dick. That's what Adrian assumed. Ultimately, he couldn't account for Danny and what he was capable of. He could only imagine the rage building inside that man sitting out there in his car for several hours each day, watching Adrian's house, waiting for him to come or go so that he could launch his attack, all the while cultivating a special brand of hate.

In the moments when Adrian was both sober and honest he admitted that Danny's strategy was working a treat. He expected to find something at some time – a bag of rotten meat on his doorstep, graffiti on his garage, or at least another note – to increase the intimidation. To debilitate Adrian's movements while the case was being prepared and charges tallied down at the station. Or, at worst, as a prelude to the physical reprisal to come. The guy had been out there for hours and hours now over the past three days, since Adrian's first day out of hospital. He'd just about had enough.

When Adrian had taken the edge off with a few drinks, he fancied his chances against the guy and his scare tactics. After seeing Rafiq yesterday he'd been drinking harder, and it was in this brazen state of mind that Adrian looked out past the curtain to see Danny Bowman sitting in his car, the window half-down. He decided to approach him.

'What the fuck are you waiting for?'

It was a stupid way to start things off, Adrian knew, leaning against his brick mailbox – casual-aggressive.

Bowman wound his window up, but Adrian could still make out his head, his face. Even if he couldn't see the man's eyes, he knew they were fixed on him.

'Chickenshit! Come out,' he yelled. 'Come on, get out of

your car if you've got something to say to me. Hey! I know who you are. I know your name, buddy. Don't think I don't recognise you.'

The more Adrian said, the more he felt like going on, but he was fast running out of things to say without the scenario devolving into something downright ugly. He was wishing Bowman would say or do something. For him to be provoked into acting rashly, recklessly. Adrian was on the verge of no longer giving a shit about himself. If Akker was intent on completely screwing his life, then he'd go out in spectacular fashion.

But then he thought he saw movement in the back of the car. It could have been a reflection, a trick of the eye – nothing at all – but it could have been Alex. Perhaps his father had forced him to join his little stakeout mission and witness firsthand how pathetic the monster had become. Perhaps it was a lesson in confronting the aggressor, the perpetrator. Putting the monster in its place. As a father, Adrian understood this. He often had to show Tam that the figure in the dark was not what he thought it was – that what he feared was just in his imagination. Because there is no creature lurking in the quiet spaces of the house. No goblin, no beast. The only true terror is the person who impresses their will upon another. This was the most sobering thought of all.

Adrian now stood upright and looked away from the Camry. He'd done his dash – for the time being, at least. As he turned to go back inside a car pulled into his driveway, and for a moment he believed some looming horror was about to strike. He felt the old heat come back to his throat when he saw who it was.

★

Sometimes all he wants to do is hit Noel in the face, shout down on him, then offer him a hand to pull him from the ground and move on. Sometimes he convinces himself he'd prefer to not talk about it – that he doesn't want answers to questions like *why?* The reasons don't exactly mean all that much in those heated moments. All he wants to hear is confirmation that, yes, it did actually happen, that it wasn't a dream or a false memory, that they were just two boys and one was six years older than the other, and that one day the older brother had ideas, and because no one else knew about those ideas no one could stop him from doing them. He created or took advantage of opportunities when no one else was around so he could get what he wanted.

The younger brother had to be taught what to do, of course, so a set of instructions was created.

I'll tap you on the head as a secret message. One tap means your teeth are hurting me so you'll have to open your mouth as big as you can. Just like this, see? And two taps means I think someone's coming, like if I hear a sound or something, so move away and pretend to be doing something else, like playing. Okay? You understand? Good boy.

Adrian doesn't want someone to blame – it isn't about that. Noel was twelve, thirteen. Kids do stuff – he knows that. Kids experiment, kids explore their sensory worlds. Kids are just trying to make sense of what they've been presented with while their bodies roil through youth. Yet Adrian still needs something – if not blame, then at least reconciliation. A ceasefire. It had to be that. A cessation of heat and fire.

Yes, no more fire.

No more fire.

Please.

★

'Little bro, look at you.' Noel hugged him there on the front lawn.

Adrian caught his breath as he felt the thickness of his brother's upper body. He wasn't so solid last time they'd stood face to face, when Noel was Adrian's best man. 'What are you doing here?'

Noel gave a knowing laugh and said, 'Brother, you know that better than any of us.'

Of course. The arithmetic was simple: Adrian's in deep shit, plus Glenda knows, plus big brother is a cop. Noel would equal the hero in this gritty quest for justice.

Noel shut the car door. 'Let's talk inside, eh?'

'Yep,' Adrian said, then took one more glance back at the Camry. Bowman had his window down again.

Noel caught the look. 'Who's ya mate over there?'

Adrian wasn't ready for that conversation. He was still making up his mind about how to react to Noel being here. 'Don't worry about that guy,' he replied. 'Not yet, anyway.'

Inside, Noel went about opening curtains and windows as though he owned the place. 'Reminds me of when you used to stay home sick from school. I always had to open up the house when I got home in the afternoon. Used to give me the shits.'

'Yeah, I remember.' *I remember heaps of stuff, actually*, he felt like saying.

Noel went into the kitchen and made a couple of coffees, then brought them out to the lounge room. 'Your nose's seen better days.'

Adrian nodded, took his coffee and sipped.

'So who is he?'

There was no mucking about with Noel. 'Just a kid at school. One of my students.'

'No, I mean the guy in the Camry. I'm guessing he's not security detail.'

'He's more like insecurity, actually. He's the kid's father.'

Noel drank audibly, nodded. 'Impressive. No wonder Mum said to come as soon as we could.'

'Are Wendy and the girls here?'

'Not my idea. They're over at Mum's, but we're staying at a hotel in Parra.'

Adrian put his head into his hands. He abruptly imagined himself up on a stand, his head locked into a guillotine, his entire family there to watch.

'We're not here to kick your tyres, mate. It might seem that way but, trust me, it's not like that.'

'Okay. It's okay.'

Noel put his hand on Adrian's shoulder; his instinct was to buck it off. That heat again. He let the hand stay.

'So has this kid's dad done or said anything to you?'

Adrian thought of the note, torn up then put back together with tape.

'I'll show you,' he said, and went and got it from his study drawer.

Noel took it, read it. 'Right,' he said. 'So what are we going to do about this fuckwit?'

★

'Leave it to me,' he said. 'Stay in the car. Don't get out.'

'Noel.'

'What?'

'Please don't let this get out of control. I don't need any more shit on my doorstep. I'm dealing with enough as it is.'

'It'll be fine. I'm just going to have a bit of a word with him. That's all.'

'Please.'

'And if it goes pear-shaped, it's on me, not you. I'll testify to that. Just stay in the fucking vehicle. If you're seen out here then you are in the shit.'

They'd tailed Danny back to the apartment block and watched him go up to his unit. It was just Danny, it turned out: Alex hadn't been in the car. Adrian didn't want to have anything to do with the whole escapade but Noel insisted that what Danny was doing was against the law, and Noel wanted to let him know. 'Just as a warning. Nothing too aggressive. Tit for tat.'

'I still don't know about this,' Adrian said. 'I'm not supposed to go anywhere near their family. This is seriously bad news if the whole thing goes to court.'

'Mate, you can't live like this, with some pumped-up dickhead stalking you in his crapbox Camry.'

'I don't have much of a life left anyway. Think about it, Noel.' He could barely believe he was defending Danny against the terror of his own brother. 'Just leave the guy alone. He'll bugger off. He'll get tired of sitting out there, and—'

'And that's when he'll come after you. He'll step out of that car and onto your driveway and he'll do something drastic. I mean, holy fuck, I'm doing the right thing by both of you here, so *you* think about it, Adrian. The guy's pissed at what you did or didn't do, or however the fucking story goes, and he's not about to forget that and come for a kiss and a cuddle. Now, let me handle this – it's why I'm here and it's what I know. I deal with grubs all the time, and I've gotta be good for something around here. Not just opening curtains and making a fucking cuppa.'

Noel was on edge, a pumped-up dickhead himself, Adrian saw, but he couldn't argue. He was hopeless at arguing at the best of times, and loathed confrontation. For a man of many words in the classroom, he was often caught bereft when he needed them most. Fight or flight? He was one of the world's best pilots.

'Okay,' he said. 'I agree. Do it.'

'Good boy.'

NOEL

Knock, knock.

Danny Bowman opened his door and Noel didn't hesitate: he put his shoulder into it and forced the door wide. He then stepped in and pressed his forearm into Danny's chest, and used his other hand to turn the guy flat against the door. Danny shouted, 'Who the fuck are y—' and didn't put up much of a fight, but Noel exercised caution and put him in a neck restraint anyway, compressing his carotid arteries. 'Don't resist,' he told him. 'Don't resist and you won't lose consciousness.'

Danny breathed heavily against the wood of the door, rapidly at first but then, after a minute, with the blood flow to his brain restricted, he calmed. Noel pulled him away and shut the door with his boot, then marched the man over to an armchair. There were no dangerous objects at hand.

'I'm going to soften my grip now and ask you to comply,' he told Danny. 'If you agree to comply I'll release and step away, at which point you must sit in the chair. You got me? Don't do anything stupid or I will use force.'

Danny grunted.

'Okay. I'm softening my grip now' – he did so – 'and I ask if you comply with my instructions.'

Danny nodded as best he could.

'Say it.'

'Yeah, I comply – yes.'

Noel let him go and stepped back. He noticed a mobile phone on the coffee table but watched Danny in the armchair, rubbing his throat. Noel lowered himself into a chair on the other side of the small table, then leant forward and picked up the mobile and put it in his pocket.

Danny watched. 'So I don't call the cops, ay?'

'I am a cop, you dickhead.'

'My arse you are.'

'No bullshit, my friend.'

'If you were a cop you'd be worried about more than just a phone.'

'Cops worry about a lot of things, including people like you and the threat they pose to others in the community.'

'I'm no threat. I've done nothing to you. I don't even know you. You're the fucken threat, mate, bashing me against the fucken door … If you really are a cop then you better get ready for a court case – your face on the telly.'

'I'm not here to bully you, Mr Bowman. What just happened there was for my own safety, because I know you better than you think, and I have reason to believe that you're actively intimidating with intent to cause fear of physical and mental harm.'

'Harm who?'

'You know exactly who I'm referring to.'

'Tell me. You think you know, so you tell me.'

'Where have you been over the past few days?'

'I go to work, I come home, go to work. I visit my kids. Drop by the bottle-o every few days. That's it: work and the unit and kids. You got kids?'

'And where else?'

'Nowhere else.'

'Is that your grey Camry parked outside?'

'Yep.'

'Then how come I've received reports that that same vehicle has been parked outside the home of your son's English teacher over the past few days?'

'That son of a bitch?'

'Excuse me?'

'He's a fucken sicko. He's the one you should be arresting.'

'Are you aware that stalking is illegal? That you can't just follow a person about or hang around in the vicinity of a person's place of residence?'

Danny sat forward now. He took a long look at Noel, then pointed at his face. 'I know who you are.'

'You've also made a written threat, which can be used as evidence against you.'

'I saw you this morning outside his house. You're family, ay? His brother?'

'Did you know that you can get up to five years in prison for that offence?'

'It's cool, mate. I get it. Family's important to you. You come here and put me into the door and choke me, take my phone.'

'I'm doing you a favour, Mr Bowman. This is a warning. Do you understand what I'm saying?'

'Especially your kids, ay? They're important to you. What

have you got – a boy, a little girl? Family's important to me too, and that's why I make sure no one harms my kids. Your family hurt my family – you get that? And now you come here and make threats against me. Did your brother say what he did to my boy? Ay? You think about your son and what you'd do if some sicko put his hands on him, put his dick in him. Eat shit, mate. My son's just a boy. You think about that. Get the fuck out of my house and get in your fucken car and think about that, and ask yourself if it's okay for someone to do those things to a boy. Ay? Ask yourself.'

Noel knew this guy was getting the edge on him. He wasn't going to let that happen. Adrian didn't need that to happen, and his little brother was the only reason he was in this stinking shithole of an apartment. Only God knew how much Adrian still had to endure, and Noel had to be the big brother for a change. That's what their mother had said: 'Be a good big brother.' Adrian didn't need this turkey hassling him.

Noel stood and Danny sat back, readying for another physical onslaught.

'Look, buddy, let the police deal with the allegations and cut this other crap out. If family's so important to you, then I'm telling you, prison's a lot worse than what you've got going here. If you want to be with your family then be with them. Don't try to be the hero.'

Noel took the phone from his pocket and slapped it on the table. He walked to the door, opened it and left without shutting it behind him.

When he got back to the car Adrian asked what happened, how it went, but Noel had to collect himself. He looked at the 'No smoking' sticker on the dash and thought, *Fuck you, hire car company, and your fucking clauses.* His hands trembled as he lit a cigarette, then he drew on it with urgency, held his breath for a moment and blew the smoke out the window. Adrian was staring at him, looking at his knuckles for evidence of carnage.

'Is he alright?' Adrian said.

'I'll take you home, tell you along the way.' Noel started the engine. 'There's something I've gotta do.'

★

After dropping Adrian off, Noel pulled into a service station car park and went inside the store. He searched the shelves until he found a street directory and turned the pages until he located what he wanted. He then tracked the easiest route, memorised it and put the book back. He went to the counter and bought a box of matches and a newspaper, then got going.

Danny Bowman's words had stung deeper than he'd anticipated. He had to do something about it now, before the sting turned into a stab and he did something foolish. And burning wasn't a foolish act – on the contrary, it was an act of cunning.

He had to be more vigilant here. Sydney had changed so much since he'd left for the west coast. He drove through areas that had been open land or bush and were now suburban estates. The houses crammed onto small blocks had been built without eaves, he noticed – anything to gain extra interior space. After thirty minutes driving south-west, he turned off the M7 and pulled up at the place he'd seen in the directory – a nature reserve where the only nearby structure was an electricity substation, and the residential area was well enough away. There was no one in sight.

Noel got out of the car and had a look about. The grass was well dry, and conditions were perfect – any later in the year and he'd be creeping into fire season. He could tell there'd been a backburn here at least a couple of years ago, so hopefully it wouldn't get out of control. He wanted it contained. Nothing too big. Just a small hit to appease.

He collected some grass and leaf litter and laid it out on the newspaper on the passenger seat. He then wrapped the matchbox and tied it all up with a long stalk of grass. The device in his hand, he shut the car door and set off into the scrub with the ease of a man far less burdened than Noel Pomeroy.

*

There was this one time when they were young that Adrian got the jump on him.

A new kid had moved in next-door – a redhead, heaps of freckles. He was nice enough, fourteen years old. Noel was almost sixteen and Adrian ten, but the kid was tall for his age. He didn't have siblings so he ended up coming around a fair bit, after school when Glenda and Mal weren't home from work, and on weekends. After a while he got on Noel's nerves a bit, so Noel started ignoring him, finding other stuff to do instead. A few times the kid knocked on the door, and when no one answered he just went away. But one day he just opened the door and walked straight into the house.

There was some talk – Noel couldn't remember exactly – and somehow they ended up out the front. There was push and shove, probably some choice words. He remembered the kid saying stuff like 'Just hit me' and 'Go on' and 'You reckon you're such a tough man'. But Noel wouldn't be goaded. The kid kept it up, then pushed Noel against the fibro and called him a pussy, said he didn't have the guts to have a go at him. Noel remembered telling the kid to just go home, over and over, while he kept saying, 'Hit me, hit me.'

Noel had forgotten about his little brother, who must have been there as witness, listening to the back and forth and waiting for his big brother to snap. Adrian must have understood that he wouldn't, because next thing Noel saw was Adrian's knuckles come up and around to smack the kid's jaw, the angle and jolt of it enough to put the kid on the ground. He remembered the kid crying and going home.

Nothing else happened. The visits stopped. But Noel didn't care so much about the hit itself – what he understood was that Adrian had a different breaking point. That Adrian was made of different stuff. He admired his brother more after that day, and while Noel continued to play the big brother role he'd inherited, he knew that Adrian was capable of more than he let on, and that he would forever be the stronger.

RILEY

Riley saw his father's flaws – his need to control, his intolerance for backchat from his kids – and played towards them whenever possible, just to see what reaction he could get. But coming out as a boy wasn't part of that play. Coming out as a boy wasn't a goad or a prank or anything; it was innate. Being a boy felt like the most natural thing he'd ever done, and yet getting other people to understand and accept this was the most fraught.

Riley knew there were only fleeting moments when his father didn't hold Riley's decision against him, but he suspected the Pomeroy family dinner might bring out the best and worst. After all, his dad was a cop, and Riley had broken his dad's own law about what a man should be. Taking the piss seemed part of that law – it was Noel's go-to whenever he couldn't make head or tail of something. And he definitely couldn't make head or tail of his second-born child ever since Riley had stopped being his little girl, the daughter he tickled and put on his shoulders and swung around doing helicopters, all those typical things dads apparently did with their little girls. Now all that had changed, according to Noel. It was as though

Riley's change of gender had somehow altered their personal histories.

When it came to the family dinner, Riley only hoped that whatever was going on with his uncle might hold centre stage, and so take some of the heat off him. No one had bothered to tell Riley and Grace what was going on exactly, but they'd put together enough bits of conversation to know that Adrian was in the shit with the police over something he'd said or done to a boy from the school he worked at. Grace said she didn't really care what was going on because she had enough going on with a boy online. But Riley, who admitted he didn't really know his uncle all that much, although he knew he liked him, wondered if Adrian had become a rejected man. Rejection was something Riley knew well.

In the plane on the way over he'd asked his mother who actually knew about his transgender status and what had been said; the answer was nobody and nothing. This was obvious when they got to Merrylands and sat in the lounge room, with its lacy curtains, brown swirly carpet and corduroy armchairs – the house was seriously stuck in the seventies. Then there were the patchwork blankets, and a collection of elephant figurines arranged in a glass cabinet in the corner.

Grandma Glenda asked why Riley's hair was so short and why he was dressed in black. Was he going to a rock concert? She then handed out gifts. Riley got a lavender-coloured T-shirt with a cartoon cat on the front with sequins for eyes. Wendy gave him a sympathetic smile. Riley said, 'Thanks, Grandma,' then quietly asked his mum when she'd finally say something. Wendy took Glenda aside straight after the gift-giving ceremony. He couldn't hear what was said, but Glenda came out of the kitchen looking flustered. She took the shirt back, clutched Riley to her side, kissed him on the head and walked back into the kitchen. And that was it.

Grandpa Mal was easier. Riley didn't know what his deal was but he seemed to have old person's disease because he just assumed Riley was his grandson anyway.

'What's your name, George?' he'd said.

Mal was sitting in his spot at the table out the back, already into his grappa. Noel stood on the lawn with a glass in one hand and a smoke in the other, watching warily.

Wendy came out. 'It's Riley, Mal. You remember our son Riley.'

Something twigged in Mal's memory. 'I don't remember you being such a good-looking lad. You've got your uncle's looks.'

Riley waited for the question, the one that always followed, but it didn't come.

'Last time you were here you kicked a soccer ball around the yard the whole time,' Mal went on. 'Couldn't get you away from the bloody thing.'

The last time Riley was here, he reckoned, he was about five. Back when his mum was doing his hair in plaits.

'And he still kicks like a girl,' Grace quipped.

Riley shot her a death stare. He had an urge to rub his forearm, the nervous twitch he always got in trouble for, but she'd only feed off that.

'You' – Wendy pointed at Grace – 'inside to help with the washing up, please.'

Grace stood, and when her mother's back was turned she stuck her finger up at Riley. Noel saw and said, 'Oi,' stamping his cigarette butt into the grass.

Later, Grace bailed Riley up when no one was around. 'Mum won't always be there to save you,' she said.

'Fuck off, Grace.'

'Why does she hardly let you out of sight? Oh, I forgot — suicide watch.'

'Seriously, fuck off.'

'You know, if you want to be a man some day you'll have to learn to stick up for yourself.'

Grace was a better bitch, but Riley would always have the intellectual advantage. 'And if you want to be a decent human being some day you'll have to do more than just stick up for yourself,' he shot back.

Grace poked her tongue out. That was the best she could do.

★

Riley was twelve when he told his parents. Twelve was young, but there were more and more transgendered youth these days. He'd done some reading online before he told them, partly because he wanted to be able to reassure them that he wasn't completely alone, and partly because he wanted to reassure himself.

When he sat them down and just came out and said it — he didn't want to show any hesitation — Noel let slip an ambiguous laugh, like disbelief mixed with mockery. Wendy looked at her former daughter as though he'd stabbed her in the womb.

'And don't blow it off by saying you always wanted a son,' Riley said, trying to lighten the mood and perhaps soften the shock. But both parents were silent. Disturbingly so. 'Please say something,' Riley said. 'Mum?'

'We're just taking it in, darling.' She shook her head. 'You've had time.'

Wendy then pulled him in close, kissed his cheek and held him to her.

'This is a fucken joke,' Noel mumbled. He got up, grabbed his keys out of the bowl by the door and drove off.

Riley fought back an urge to cry. It was all too much. It was a massive relief to have finally said what had to be said, but he also felt guilty for making his mum and dad upset. The little girl he knew was still in there – still a part of him, though unreal at the same time – wanted to cry into her mum's chest and take it all back. But there was no taking it back now, so he just cried, and so did his mum as she said, 'I'll love you any which way.'

Noel didn't come home until late. Riley heard him pull into the driveway, the front door clunk and the keys clink back in the bowl. Wendy had been waiting up. There was murmuring in the lounge room. Riley got out of bed and listened at the door. He knelt down and lay on the carpet, ear to the light sliding beneath. The murmuring was clearer, enough for him to follow the conversation.

'—mental health problem,' he heard his mother say.

'Well, it's not my fault, is it? I wasn't too rough with her when she was young?' His dad did like to play rough-and-tumble games when Riley was a little kid, swinging him around, play-wrestling, but of course that had nothing to do with it.

'I think it's more complicated than that.'

'What about kids at school? They'll tease the shit out of her.'

'I don't know. These things are apparently more accepted these days.'

'It's fucken embarrassing is what it is. I can't be seen in the street with her if she's prancing around all—'

'Noel, come on.'

'What?'

'Well, she's had short hair for a while now, and she wears fairly masculine clothes, I guess. She's never been into dresses.'

'But there's a difference between that—'

'I know, but—'

'Does it mean she's into girls now or what?'

Riley got up from the floor then – he didn't want to hear any more of it. Grace had asked this last question straight-out when he told her. And he told her first, because he needed backup if things didn't go well with their parents.

'Does that make you a lesbian guy?' Grace said. 'Coz that's really weird.'

'No,' he replied. 'I think I still like guys.'

'So you're … a homo girl? That's just as freaky-deaky, dude.'

Kids at school were mostly okay with it. Public schools were good for that. Some idiots said he was next-level cringe, but he'd been wearing shorts and shirts for about a year and his best friend said most people thought he was just a bit of a try-hard, being weird on purpose, so they didn't pay all that much attention.

But Riley was mature and intelligent enough to understand he had to give his family time and space to get their heads around it. He figured that if he showed them respect in this way, then sooner or later they would realise he was the one who needed support through this, not them. And 'this' wasn't a phase. This was a decision he felt only had to be made on a superficial level, on an outward level, because beneath the surface there was no choice. He'd had no clear-cut moment of epiphany – it was more like being in the back seat and arriving at the destination he supposed he would reach sometime.

He just got closer and closer to the idea, until he felt comfortable and confident enough to let the idea become him. In retrospect, it was inevitable.

Yet he also knew his body was actively betraying him. Although he was still flat-chested he could feel his breasts developing, so he started binding, at least to get used to the feeling of constriction, and the sweating in summer. He began a routine of doing push-ups each morning to build his upper body, and borrowed Grace's laptop and sat in his bedroom to search websites and blogs about puberty blockers – how people felt about using them and how they worked.

He wasn't keen on the phrase *gender dysphoria* because it sounded more like a problem than a thing, but that was the term used for people like him. He knew that one day soon he'd have to talk to his parents about seeing a doctor and a psychologist and a psychiatrist to get the process going, but he also knew they wouldn't buy into it for a while. At least until they were convinced that it wasn't a phase, just being trendy or whatever, something he'd grow out of.

In the meantime, he watched for indications. Perhaps he'd know it was time when his dad stopped making jokes about him not being a real man until he could pee standing up, or about finally having another male in the family to complain about all the oestrogen, or about watching the footy down the pub with the rest of the blokes. Perhaps he'd know it was time when his mother didn't look at him as though she'd birthed a monstrosity. Perhaps he'd know it was time when his family again looked at him with the recognition that he was one of them – a Pomeroy – not some deranged imposter with deviant tendencies.

He hoped that the Sydney trip might somehow bring about this last possibility – that by spending more time with other Pomeroys he might find his place in the pack. No longer outside it. A change was on the cards – he could feel it – but he had no idea what that change would resemble. All he knew was that he wanted to go back to Perth more sure about who he was, and who he could become.

★

The Pomeroy family dinner began as expected, with Glenda's lip-kissing by the front door and Mal's nod.

'The circus is in town,' Mal said, and Riley was the only one to laugh. He didn't understand his father's constant grumbles about Grandpa. Riley liked his grandfather's niggly comments, the jibes. He saw in him only the old man softened by the side-effects of homebrew, not the father who once upon a time was deft at wielding a belt. Grandma Glenda had grown on Riley too – within two days he became familiar with the sound of her movements as she bustled between fridge and counter and sink and bin. The tedium of her sighs and grunts of small effort. The click of knees and lick of fingertips. These were the aspects of a person you couldn't know by just talking on the phone on birthdays and at Christmas and every so often.

At the beginning of the night all the ladies were in the kitchen, breaking open store-bought roast chickens and bagged salad. The inevitable potato bake was in the oven, which Glenda said she made because it was Adrian's favourite. Nguyet made *cha gio* and *goi ga*.

'Yikes,' Grace said, joining Riley and Tam in the lounge room. 'Bit crazy in there.'

Tam was lying on the corduroy sofa, checking out the games on Riley's phone.

Grace sat next to Riley on the carpet. 'Bro, you look weird tonight,' she said.

'Please …'

'No, I'm serious. You look different somehow.'

Truth was, Riley didn't feel himself. His emotions were amplified, and his guts hurt like someone had their hands in there and was mucking about with his intestines. He wondered whether it had something to do with his uncle. He was looking forward to seeing Adrian. But Riley had anxiety a lot and it didn't always need a reason.

'Do you feel different?' Grace continued.

'A bit,' he said. 'Hey Tam, when's your dad getting here?'

Tam shrugged.

'Like, how different?'

'Grace, leave it alone, okay?'

'I'm not trying to be a bitch. This time.'

'That'd be a change.'

'She swore,' Tam said, his face still in the phone. 'I know how to swear in Vietnamese.'

'Really?' Grace sat up. 'Give us your best one.'

'*Doi la cho de.*'

Riley and Grace laughed a bit.

'What does that mean?' Riley said.

Tam looked up and grinned. 'Life's a son of a bitch.'

All three cracked up.

'My mum says that sometimes. When she's really mad. She says Vietnamese don't like swearing so they don't have many swear words.'

'Yeah, well, I don't even reckon that should count as swearing,' Riley said, 'because sometimes life really is a son of a bitch.'

'What's all this about bitches?'

Adrian was standing in the doorway – he'd slipped in while everyone else was outside.

'Hey, Dad,' Tam said, monotone, not looking up.

'Miss me?'

'Nup,' Tam said.

Adrian feigned a growl and came over to the lounge, grabbing the boy around his waist, then lifting him upside-down into the air. Tam giggled as the phone dropped onto the sofa and his pants slid a little. As did Adrian's grip. Tam squealed.

'I got you, buddy,' Adrian said, then righted the boy and held him to his chest. 'I wouldn't lose you that easily.'

Glenda came in and hugged Adrian, commenting on his nose, which had a thin strip of gauze taped across it. The two of them then went out the back. Riley got up and followed. He stood at the doorway and watched his uncle do the rounds – more awkward hugs and polite words. Adrian looked at Riley a couple of times, over shoulders.

Mal poured an extra grappa and Adrian sat at the table, and they all started talking about stuff Riley had no interest in. Everyone seemed a bit uneasy. Even from the doorway Riley sensed some great big knot at the table that no one was brave enough to untie. He knew that sometimes things were better left that way, though the hurt was clear on all their faces. Despite the drinks they sipped on. Despite the food Grandma Glenda and Nguyet were carting out to the table.

Riley turned inside.

★

Adrian collected dishes and cutlery and Glenda said not to worry, that it was her job, that he should just relax, but he told her to sit and he'd take care of cleaning up. Nguyet was fussing over what Tam had and hadn't eaten yet, and Grace was back in the lounge room watching TV. Mal and Noel were talking about the work still needing to be done on the kit car, which Riley assumed was the thing under the blue tarp behind the garage. And Wendy was giving a fair amount of attention to her wine glass, getting pretty pissy.

Riley rubbed his stomach. It felt bloated, and the fingers were in his intestines again, having a dig, so he got up and took his plate to the kitchen. Adrian was running water in the sink when he walked in and put his plate on the counter.

'So, how's it all going?' Adrian said.

'It's okay.'

'I mean the trans stuff. Sorry, your mum mentioned it earlier – I hope that's okay.'

Riley shrugged.

'So how is it, with your mum and dad and everything? They coping?'

'Sometimes it's hard to tell if we really are one big happy family, or if we're all just trying really hard to make it look that way.'

'I know what you mean.'

Riley nodded. 'I get the impression things are a bit shitty for you at the moment.'

'I'll say. But hey, it brought you here so I guess it's not all that shitty.'

Riley smiled, but felt his guts churn again. He held his stomach.

'Toilet's down there,' Adrian pointed out.

Riley went to go.

'And hey, if you just be yourself, they'll come around eventually.'

'Yeah. I hope you're right,' Riley said, and Adrian went back to the dishes.

Riley went down the hallway. Along the walls were framed family portraits – photos of Noel and Adrian when they were young boys, then as teenagers, and one of each with their wives and kids. And Grandpa Mal was right, Riley did share some of his uncle's features: he could see it in the shape of the eyes, lips and nose. It was especially evident in the photos of Adrian around the same age as Riley was now.

Then Riley looked at their family photo. He normally avoided looking at photos like this – at the little girl he'd been not all that long ago. The truth was that little girl did know happiness, and knew it well. He wondered when she'd lost that capacity for delight, the sense of ease within herself. Before doubt was seeded. Before the frustration, the resentment coming from some place inside she couldn't locate.

Riley shut the toilet door but took grief in with him. And when he sat he looked down, and what he saw made him shudder and cry so hard he had to lift his shirt and hold it in a bunch against his mouth.

It all broke in on him in that one moment. He screamed into the cloth.

★

'You've been in there ages, bro.' Grace knocked gently on the door. She must have heard Riley sobbing.

He tried to clear his voice to make it sound normal, but it was alarmingly girlish. 'Where's Mum?'

'She went for an ice cream run. Why?'

'I won't come out unless Mum's here.'

'Why, what's wrong? Have you been chucking up in there or something? Have you crapped your pants?'

'Grace, why do you have to be such an arsehole?'

Grace went quiet for a moment, then apologised.

'I said I need Mum. Can you call her mobile and ask her to hurry up?'

'I'm seriously worried now, okay? Can you just let me help you, just this once? I swear I'll never offer to help again.'

Riley folded some toilet paper and wiped the wetness from his face as much as he could. He stood and got himself ready, then opened the door. Grace looked at him, then around the toilet. She pulled him in close. 'What is it? Tell me.'

*

By the time they went out the back and tried to make it look as though nothing had happened, Mal and Noel were showing clear signs of being drunk.

'Now, what's your name, George?' Mal said. He was looking at Riley, standing with Grace in the doorway.

Noel squinted at Riley through a smoke and grappa haze. 'It's Riley. You know that, Grandpa,' he said.

'You know, the last time you were here I swear that bloody soccer ball was glued to your friggin' foot.' Mal laughed. In front of him on the table was a giant bottle, almost empty.

'And look at her now, eh?' Noel slurred. 'She's a beauty, isn't she?'

Riley stared at his dad so Noel stared back. Riley looked away.

'What?' Mal said, though it was less a word than a snort.

'Dad ...' Grace piped up.

'But she is, though, isn't she? Even dressed up like a dyke.'

'Dad, don't—'

'She can't piss standing up, though, can ya?'

Riley began scratching his arm. He fought back tears.

'Not now, Dad,' Grace urged. 'Please.'

'This conversation's got me friggin' beat,' Mal said.

'Why not now, eh? She got her period or something?'

Grace looked at Riley, now scratching his arm like crazy. He met Grace's eyes and a sob cracked from his mouth.

'Holy hell, is that right?' Noel went on. 'That's just too funny.' Then he clapped and laughed so hard he started coughing. Soon he could no longer breathe.

Riley wanted nothing more than for that to happen.

FOUR

FOUR

ADRIAN

Adrian stood at his mother's kitchen sink, tipsy, but he'd been careful not to go over the limit. He was saving himself for an escape of a different kind, and the time was fast approaching.

Wendy came in. Her heavy-lidded eyes said she'd been going harder on the drink, which was unlike the Wendy he'd known. She leant against the brown laminate benchtop. Her body seemed loose; the tension had dropped out of her.

'Pomeroy conversation no longer pleasing you either?' he asked. In the window, against the dark outside, he watched Wendy's reflection.

She shook her head, pulled her glass to her mouth but didn't sip. 'Not sure I've ever been pleasured by a Pomeroy.' She spoke over the rim of wine, her eyes sliding to some thought.

Adrian kept at the dishes. 'Maybe I'm the wrong Pomeroy you should be talking to about that kind of thing.'

Wendy made a sound of distaste. 'Talk? To my charming husband?'

Adrian raised an eyebrow at the reflection. 'Then perhaps that's something you should talk to Noo about. God knows you'd have a better chance of talking to her than I do at the moment.'

'No, I don't think so. Not at all.'

'And everyone else out there wants to say something to me but nobody's game. Everybody's skirting the fucking obvious.'

She sipped the wine, then cradled it against her chest. 'I don't care what's being said or not said, Adrian. You're just a person, and people sometimes do things that don't make sense until you dig a bit further, like acting on desires they didn't know they had. Our actions are a strange sequence of events, sometimes. I mean … *did* you do it?'

Adrian considered his response. He rinsed a cup. 'It's complicated.'

'See? That's exactly what I'm talking about.' She took another sip, only deeper. 'Look, I don't go around telling this to anyone, but Noel has never' – she lowered her voice, almost theatrically – 'he's never made me orgasm. Not once, believe it or not.'

Adrian had no idea what to say to that.

'Can you imagine what that's like? I mean, I'm convinced I married a fucking teenage boy sometimes. He just takes what he wants, then gets up and leaves for a cigarette or for work, and if I'm lucky I'll get some stupid text message later. I thought I was marrying an astronaut – you know, attached to the mother ship – but it turns out he's a fucking cowboy.'

Adrian understood. Noel appeared to be the giving kind – the upright cop, going out of his way for others, putting himself in harm's way for strangers – but this masked a selfishness beyond anything Adrian had seen in another person.

'I'm sure you're not like that,' Wendy continued. 'I'm sure Nguyet's quite happy in that department.'

'You're not propositioning me, are you?' It was half a joke. 'Because you know I like boys now.'

She prodded his backside with a foot. 'Don't be a dickhead as well as a paedophile.'

They both laughed. It was good to laugh like that. It'd been a while.

Adrian finished the last dish, put it in the rack and pulled the plug. He turned to face her. She was more gratifying in the flesh. 'Do you want to come for a drive? There's something I need to do.'

'Not me on the back seat, I assume.'

He hoped his expression said: *Please, enough of that.* 'We could say we're buying the kids some ice cream or something.'

Now Wendy was raising an eyebrow at him.

*

They pulled up at a small park adjacent to a two-storey house. The park had a swing set, a slide and a climbing apparatus.

Wendy leant forward, looked. 'Is this a regular thing now?'

They'd shared a joint only one other time, the night before his wedding.

'I try not to make a habit of it,' Adrian said, texting on his mobile.

Next moment a window on the top floor of the two-storey house slid open and a kid clambered out onto the roof. He eased himself from the guttering onto the side fence, a tall corrugated-iron job, and jumped to the ground. Hood up, he walked over to the swings.

'Here's my guy,' Adrian said. He opened the car door and walked across the road to meet him.

'Hey, sir.'

'Evening, Christos.'

'Double the usual, eh?'

'Yeah, mate, things might be tight for a while.'

'So I hear.' Christos looked past him to Wendy in the car. 'Plus you got company.'

Adrian turned to see Wendy, her face lit by the stereo LEDs. He liked the fact that she was along for the ride. He somehow felt safer with Wendy around. She was looking straight at the two of them.

'She's family. She's okay.'

Christos seemed fine with this, although it was difficult to see any kind of expression beneath the hoodie.

'Okay, so double the stuff is double the usual price.'

'Of course,' Adrian said.

'No sympathy discounts or nothin'.'

'Sure. And you're on a good deal with this buyer so I don't see why you'd want that to change.'

'Yeah, well, you know the price of me keeping my mouth shut about our set-up.'

'And you know that I could bring you down for dealing to the Year Ten boys on school grounds.'

Christos looked back up at his bedroom window. The light was on. No movement. He turned back around, snorted, then spat a long tendon of saliva on the swing seat beside him. 'Well, credibility and shit, hey.'

Adrian understood. Recent events had certainly deteriorated any advantage he had in this arrangement. 'Can't argue with that, I guess,' he said.

'So is it true what they're saying?'

'Depends on what's being said.'

'That you and Akker sucked each other off in the library quiet study zone.'

Adrian shook his head. Back over in the car Wendy was no longer watching. 'No, that's bullshit.'

'That's what I was thinking, sir. Actually, there's a lot of people saying the same as me. Heaps of people say Akker's making shit up.'

'Really?'

'Totally.'

This confirmed what Rafiq had said, but it also appeared Adrian had supporters.

'Interesting,' he replied.

'Yeah, well, let's do this, hey? I gotta get back inside before my mum realises and shit.'

'Sure,' he said, and passed over his cash for the baggy of weed.

★

They pulled up at a park in Holroyd. Adrian sometimes brought Tam here to ride their bikes, but tonight he and Wendy sat on the pier overlooking a duck pond with a dribbly fountain. Adrian rolled a joint, lit it and handed it to Wendy.

She drew on it gently. 'How are we going to mask the smell? Noel's going to have a fit. He can detect marijuana from a kilometre away.'

'Well, it looks like we might be putting that ability to the test tonight.'

She passed it back to Adrian, who drew hard. 'Perhaps his powers are fading,' she said. 'Something's not right with him lately.'

'Just lately? Something's always been not right with Noel … Sorry, I don't mean to disrespect your decision to marry the bloke, but as his brother I think I can say with a reasonable degree of authority that he's never exactly been settled. Sometimes he manages to create a convincing façade.'

'Don't be sorry. I mean, I love him, I'm just worried about where it's all going. He's become uncommunicative. Unless you count grunting. Which I guess you can, but it's not exactly conducive to a healthy relationship.'

Adrian drew on the spliff again. He felt the familiar warmth sweep into his lungs, his heart accelerating, yet as he exhaled, his body slowly undid itself, as though all its ligaments and tendons became elongated, supple. He passed it back. 'Did something happen on the job?' he asked. 'He must have to deal with some pretty grim stuff.'

'The very best and worst humanity can muster.'

'But was there something particularly traumatic? Maybe all that immorality just builds up after a while?'

'I don't think it's the job. It's been going on for a while. He's been disappearing from duties.'

'You don't think—'

'No, I don't think so.'

'And that's not meant to be an indictment on you.'

'Perhaps best not to go there again tonight.'

Adrian laughed. It could have been the joint or it could have been the company he was keeping.

'How's it going with Noo? The two of you aren't talking?'

'It's not going well, I can tell you that much. But it started long before these allegations. People think that because she's quiet she either doesn't speak English well or she's not as passionate as they are about stuff, but when she has a desire she certainly makes it clear – at least to me. And what she wants more than anything is simple, but complex at the same time. All she wants is another child, but it's complex because of the reason why, and also because I'm against the idea.'

Wendy pulled on the joint and blew the smoke towards the moon. 'Do you think it's a deal-breaker?'

'I don't know. I've tried talking her out of it, tried arguing that Tam's enough for us, for the world – that the world doesn't need another Pomeroy to help screw it up. But no luck. I even tried getting a dog, knowing full well that she's not keen on pets because she doesn't like the hair getting everywhere. But I read an article about the glut of animals at the local shelter and said we should take a look, help out. Tam got all excited about the idea so Noo bowed to the pressure. I knew it was an unfair substitute for what she really wanted – unfair for both the animal and Noo. Anyway, we drove to the shelter, and when we got there the dogs all barked and paraded at the front of their pens and we walked along and picked one – this terrier cross we named Cho. On the way home Noo held the dog in her lap and told me she'd eaten dog as a child, at her uncle's restaurant in Hanoi. It was a delicacy, she said, then she laughed – laughed hard – and told Cho not to worry, that she didn't like the taste anyway. I hadn't heard her laugh that way for ages.'

'That sounds like a happy thing.'

'Yeah, it was. We all liked the dog and she took a liking to me most. We put her bed in front of the bookshelf in my study, and she'd scratch around and hang out with me at night while I marked exams. Then I was rubbing her belly with my foot one night when I felt a lump with my toe. I thought it was probably a cyst so we let it go for a while, just to see if it went away by itself. It stayed like that for ages, but then one day Noo called me at work and said Cho was having some kind of fit.'

'Like a seizure?'

'Yeah. Noo was flipping out. I told her to take it to the vet straight away, and she did, but that was pretty much the end of the line for dear little Cho.'

'A tumour?'

'More than one, actually.'

'When was this? And why didn't we hear about it?'

'It was a couple of years ago. We only had her for about six months. Plus you guys are on Perth time.'

'True. Sometimes it feels like a different continent over there.'

Adrian nodded. 'You want another?' The joint was spent.

'Definitely not. I'm the wife of a police officer with a short fuse, don't you know?'

ALEX

After Adrian told him to cut out the crap that night in his car out the back of work, Akker tried to look for some new interest, some distraction. Marley was good for that. But he also made Akker aware of the tightrope he was walking.

At school one day they were hanging in their usual lunch spot under the trees at the side of the oval. Mr Pomeroy walked past and nodded to the group of boys, and as soon as he turned his back Marley was up, grabbing his groin and moving his fistful up and down.

'Come for some of this, eh, homo?' he said to Mr Pomeroy's back, but not so loud that he could actually hear. Anything for a response from his boys. 'He is such a cocksucker, that guy,' he said, turning back to them. 'I heard he wants to suck yours, Akker,' he said, wanking a fist into his open mouth, his tongue pushing against his cheek.

His mates laughed and agreed, and Akker laughed too, suppressing the need to wince. He wondered if somehow he'd unknowingly let out a word or given a look that revealed his thoughts. He felt he might throw up right there on the grass, but

Marley sat next to him and bumped him with his shoulder. 'Just grilling ya, bro,' he said. 'Don't cry about it.' Then Akker told the boys about his dad going poofter-bashing, ages ago, about what they did to those two fags that night. This took some of the heat off, but Alex knew a word for what he was feeling: *duplicity*.

Marley was new to the school that year and had edged his way into Akker's social group with bravado and cocksureness. Akker didn't mind. He recognised Marley's brand of persuasion, and the guy often amused the boys with his antics. But out of everyone in the group Marley favoured Akker the most. They riled each other a lot. Akker liked it when Marley slung an arm around his neck and walked with him. He couldn't say Marley turned him on, but he was attracted in some way to his sheer presence. Akker felt tougher around him, more capable. He felt empowered to push boundaries, to grab his dick and thrust it at the world. He was there by Marley's side when he exercised his will on the more susceptible students – the younger ones, the geeky ones, the ones whose bodies were lagging behind. He laughed along with Marley at their misfortune, their idiocy, their otherness. Until one time Akker got ahead of himself and made an error, a game-changer which turned the tormenter's gaze back towards him. This was to set in motion a machine Akker hadn't contemplated.

It happened in the change rooms after a game of soccer for physical education class. The boys were showering and Akker was one of the last in. 'Hurry up, you guys!' he yelled. 'Stop hogging the showers.'

'You can come in here,' Marley said over the hiss of showers. 'As long as you don't mind getting shamed by my huge one.' Some of the guys laughed.

The boys all showered in underpants, but when Akker opened the cubicle door he saw Marley standing under the running water completely naked. Akker latched the door and, as he took his own clothes off, couldn't help glancing at Marley with his eyes closed under the stream of water. Akker removed his underpants too.

'Hurry up, it's freezing out here,' he said.

'Just get under and I'll get out,' Marley said.

So he did. But Marley didn't get out, not right away. And as they stood there, Akker touched him – it could have been an accidental brush with the side of his hand. When Marley didn't react he did it again, and this time his intentions couldn't be denied.

What followed was a rush. Marley swore and said he was being a fag – that only a fag would do something like that. Akker denied it but it didn't make any difference: Marley was all over it. Akker couldn't remember the exact words he used. Marley shouted and grabbed his towel and clothes, then opened the cubicle door to leave Akker exposed as the rest of the guys, drawn by the commotion, looked in and laughed at Akker, dripping in the stall with a shrinking hard-on.

'Look at the homo,' Marley yelled. 'He's a fucken homo!'

★

The fight on the oval happened not long after. Marley continued targeting Akker and news of the shower incident quickly spread. Akker was sick with anxiety, so he stayed home when his mother allowed it. Some days he just wagged. Then, the night of the fight with Marley, Akker wrote the third story for Adrian, and into that story he funnelled all the frustrations he'd experienced not only over the past weeks and months, but ever since he'd first laid eyes on the teacher. Ever since Adrian had first expressed belief in him.

When Akker sent that final story, he knew that he was broken. And that there was only one way to fix himself – to fix this situation. Deflection. He had to gain their sympathy, not their mockery. Otherwise, he didn't know how he could cope.

★

Then came the meeting with Mr H and his parents, with his father getting furious, saying the teacher would pay, and his mother saying 'my boy, my boy' over and over. Then word got around fast, especially after the police came to school and pulled students and teachers out of class for interviews.

At first people were supportive, saying how brave he was in speaking out against sexual abuse, that it must have taken guts to come forward, and that Adrian Pomeroy would get what he deserved once they carted him off to prison – because everyone knew what they did to people like him in prison. Akker basked in this. Partly because he was being lauded, but also because it suppressed the stray stones of guilt rumbling around his mind. He was recognised as the victim, and so he was able to wrest back some degree of control.

But after only a few days this feeling of control was revoked. It began with graffiti on the wall of the toilet near the English block: *Akker Bowman is a fucken liar.* Then a message scrawled on the seat at the bus stop: *Eat shit Akker you dog.* And it didn't stop there. Online, his social media accounts were hammered with posts, some championing him, others suspicious of the allegations. Once the trolling really kicked into gear, he deleted his accounts. But the final point was made loud and clear when his name and mobile phone number were written in thick black marker on the wall of the change rooms. It had been scrubbed off by the next day but the damage was done, and he received about a dozen text and voice messages saying what a piece of shit mofo hoaxer he was, that his prank wasn't funny and he was ruining other people's lives for some fucking power fantasy, and that everyone knew he was a closet gay. These people didn't know what had led to the allegations in the first place, though he doubted this would ever truly be known. He wasn't even sure he wanted the full story to be told, regardless of what his school motto advocated.

There was one voice message of support from someone he didn't recognise, but it didn't matter. He destroyed his sim card. The fact was, his anonymous supporter had it wrong and the vast majority were right. He'd been the biggest dog of all time, and what made his stomach turn the most was the thought of Adrian enduring his own tirade of abuse. No doubt his marriage was being ripped in two and his son was crying because he didn't understand why.

Akker thought more than once about going to the house again, one last time – to make sure Adrian was okay, to glimpse the wreckage he'd tolled, to comprehend the ramifications. Maybe, just maybe, there was a chance things weren't as bad as he thought. Maybe Adrian and his family were hanging tight. Maybe the police would find insufficient evidence and the case would be dismissed. All would be okay. All would be sweet and they could each go on with their lives …

But of all his fantasies he knew this to be the most elaborate and least credible. No. There was no return, no reverse gear on this machine, so there was only one thing within his power to do. Even though it would not make things go back to the way they were, this decision would at least allow him to start putting things right. This decision would be his final act of love. This final act would be his apology.

*

Akker stood in the middle of a maths lesson. His chair scraped the floor.

'Where might you be off to, Mr Bowman?' the teacher asked, but Akker ignored him and walked to the front of the room and out the door. Boys in the class were making some kind of noise but he didn't care anymore – not about them and not about the traps lurking elsewhere on the school grounds. They could all go fuck themselves.

He left his bag behind but none of that mattered. He made his way past the front administration building to the gate, where he turned and stuck his finger up at whoever might've been watching, at the school itself. He walked out the gate knowing he wouldn't be back. Not ever.

Then he ran.

He snatched at thoughts as he sped along. He thought of the way Shannon now looked at him – as though her big brother had become prey, helpless and fragile. She'd stopped teasing him, joking with him, being affectionate. Then there was his mother, who heaped on the affection, touching his hair and chest and back as though she could somehow reclaim him from what he had become, her eyes and the etched shape of her mouth speaking of the wound. She hadn't cried when she was around him, not since the meeting with Mr H, but he heard her at night in her bed. And then there was his father, whose rage bucked beneath his skin. This knowledge had not set them free, nor was this knowledge a mere blemish. This knowledge was trauma.

Akker thought of these things as he ran along the street away from the school and towards the first person he wanted to reach out to. The flat wasn't all that far. He arrived after twenty minutes or so, out of breath on the doorstep.

'Dad, are you home?'

Danny opened the door and Alex rushed into his arms.

'Mate, what's going on? What's happened?'

But Alex didn't reply. He couldn't utter a word. Not yet. First, he needed to use his father's phone.

ADRIAN

When a six-year-old boy is being coerced behind a closed door, he is capable of suspecting that what he is doing is wrong. So is the other one, the older one, although he probably knows better, should know better. Perhaps he doesn't, though. What then? Who is to blame? Who is at fault? Can fault even be attributed? The six-year-old boy doesn't know to ask these questions. These ideas are beyond his education, his cognitive development. But not beyond his experience. And so begins the conspiracy of words and actions. Whole lives pass under the conspiracy's veil. Until, at last, one of those boys asks how the veil will be finally lifted. How? How on earth?

★

Adrian woke on his parents' lounge just before six. Tam was asleep beside him, curled between him and the backrest, head on Adrian's chest. Late spring breathed through the curtains. The morning was too formative for anyone else in the house to be up, especially after last night's finale. He knew the repercussions of the evening were yet to play out – with his brother, with

Wendy coming back reeking of pot, and the bruises still there in the air from riling piss talk. He'd realised when they pulled up in the driveway that he'd completely forgotten about the ice cream, and was kind of glad that this detail, the supposed purpose of why he and Wendy had taken off in the first place, was a distant taste on everyone's lips.

But none of that was a concern for him right then. There was a decided calm to the morning, an assuredness in the filtered light and yet-to-come urban noise – stifled yawns, boiling kettles, teaspoons in cereal bowls, passing traffic. None of those impositions. Just his boy on his chest, ear to his heart, the only one to know its rhythm. And Adrian knew then that he loved his son like nothing else in the world, and it would always be so. That neither Akker nor Noel could bring a halt to such knowing. That there were certain things which couldn't be touched.

He edged himself off the lounge, placed Tam's head on a cushion, spread the long blanket along his body and smoothed it with a hand. In the kitchen he prised open the fridge door and took a guzzle of milk. When he closed the fridge he noticed on its door a photo he hadn't seen for a long time, but realised immediately how deeply its 1980s shapes and colours were embossed on his consciousness. He realised also the irony of the photo as a surface, a framed moment: that the two boys showing their happiest faces were masking something else entirely.

But Glenda knew none of that, of course, and here it was, magnetised to the fridge door like a trophy of the past. On another day he might have taken the photo and put a match to it, although he knew his mother would ask questions; if Noel had got his predisposition to policing from a genetic source, it was certainly her. But this was a day to let sleeping dogs lie.

Adrian collected his keys and wallet from the bench and went back to the lounge room to kiss his son's forehead. He then left.

He was convinced he wasn't running away: he knew he no longer had a place there, and that his wife's needs took priority. The thought of her waking to him in the house, coming from the spare room to eye him with her best attempt at downplaying her disappointment, was neither endearing nor reassuring. He figured it less confusing for the boy and his mother if he left. Rafiq was right – Noo needed space. As did he.

He got into his mother's car, started it and peeled away for home.

There were few cars on the road. This part of Sydney was only rousing, while nearby Parramatta was no doubt already abuzz with delivery trucks and small-business owners. But Adrian cruised, taking the backstreets through suburbs where families like his eked out their living, suffering with drama and tragedy, asking questions and finding few answers. Sometimes there were celebrations worth shouting for. Small triumphs. Victories. Coups. Little things to celebrate and be thankful for. This was his Sydney. These were the families whose kids he had once taken joy in teaching. Trying to convince them of the value of language, of imagination. Sharing their achievements. Kids going some place – moving forward. With pride and articulation. Finding the best words to express aspects of themselves and the world they know. These were successes worth striving for. This was something to believe in on a good morning.

★

Adrian was home for a couple of hours before some unexpected guests arrived. He'd made coffee and toast, then sorted through his novels in the study only to find the school library's copy of John Cheever, which he'd forgotten he'd borrowed that day, back with Akker in the quiet study zone. He thought of this, picked it from the shelf, then sat at the front porch table and read.

After a while he heard a car pull up, and when he lowered the book he saw Detective Inspector Fielder and a uniformed officer stepping out of a police vehicle. They walked across the lawn.

'Morning, Mr Pomeroy.' The monotone of Fielder.

An internal organ – it could have been Adrian's stomach – tightened. He knew his time was up. Of course it was – it would only go down on a good day. The authorities had done their muckraking and dredged sufficient evidence to lay charges. And Fielder wanted to be the one to do it. The guy had wanted to screw him over good and proper from the outset.

Adrian stood, but not in anger. The fight had gone out of him. Today was about surrender. In his imagination he was already holding out his wrists for cuffing.

'Officers,' he said. 'So this is it, is it?'

Fielder stopped at the bottom of the porch steps and looked up at Adrian. 'I'm not sure I completely gather your meaning, Mr Pomeroy. But I'm probably not far off the mark.'

Adrian put the book on the table. His hands shook. 'The arrest,' he said, though that dreaded word barely came out, such was the blockage in his throat.

Fielder looked at his officer, then back at Adrian. 'We need to talk. May we come in?'

★

With each passing moment his anticipation grew lighter, yet his confusion grew deeper. He directed them to the kitchen table, where they hauled out chairs and made themselves comfortable. Fielder spoke – the other didn't seem to own a voice.

'Now, we have some new information regarding the allegations. Yesterday, Mr Alex Bowman contacted the station via telephone to notify us that he's decided to drop the charges. He also attended the station late yesterday afternoon with his father to make a formal statement in this regard, and recanted his original statement.'

Adrian's guts still churned but his head instantly lightened. 'Really?'

'Yes, really. However, regardless of Mr Bowman's change of perspective, we can still proceed with charges if we believe there's a case to answer. This happens more than you might think, especially if an alleged perpetrator has made admissions of guilt or if there are independent witnesses – then the matter can proceed even without the alleged victim's cooperation.'

'Right.' Adrian felt both hopeful and decidedly grim. 'Off the hook, but still in the abattoir.'

'If you prefer to think of it in those terms, yes. It's important for you to know that we're continuing to look into the case with the Office of the Director of Public Prosecutions.'

'And when will I know if you think there's still a case to answer?'

Adrian had never made an admission of guilt, nor had there been witnesses to any action he could be charged with. He knew this. He'd been careful enough. Foolish, to say the least, but a careful fool. The best witness would be the old clerk, but nothing had even happened that night. It was too circumstantial without Alex's statement.

Holy shit – Alex. Adrian wondered what had happened to prompt this change. For better or for worse?

'It's difficult to say,' Fielder replied. 'We'll try to have an outcome as soon as possible, bearing in mind the delicacy of the circumstances.'

'And you'll keep my stuff until you have an outcome?'

'Correct. We'll continue to hold the seized property unless there's no case to answer, after which you can come collect those items from the station.'

Fielder had to remain circumspect – that was his job – but there was something in his demeanour that told Adrian he'd be okay, that they were just following procedure. Fielder's eyes sent a conciliatory message, and Adrian couldn't help but feel relief. Utter relief. Alex had granted him a reprieve. His life had been handed back to him – liberated from the train tracks of personal and professional destruction. Control had been placed back in his possession. Noo and Tam could come home. He'd get his job back. All would be sweet again. He almost felt a hankering to get back into the classroom, even to mark some papers.

Yet as he showed the officers out the front door, with Fielder saying they'd be in touch, his initial emotion dwindled and in swooped another. Guilt – which he had successfully evaded for the most part until this point. Strange that it should arrive now, he thought, now that the ordeal might soon end. So why?

Adrian remained on the porch as the police vehicle drove away. He picked up his book from the table. He stared at the cover, then looked through it, reaching out to memory, to Alex.

There – that was his guilt. The fact that Alex had been reduced to both victim and unwitting villain. It was all bullshit. Alex was neither. And Adrian was both. Alex wasn't really to blame; although he had played a part, Adrian was in the position of authority but hadn't shut the whole thing down. And he hadn't shut it down because, quite simply, he liked it. He liked Alex more than he knew he should.

As he closed up the house and got into his mother's car, Fielder's last words resounded: 'I suggest you continue to steer clear of the Bowman family. Do not approach them or their home, or the school during school hours. I understand you might feel tempted to do so, and to say something to them – I've seen it before – but don't. You'll only cause distress for all involved, and potentially incriminate yourself.'

Adrian had nodded, said he understood completely.

'There are many temptations in this world, Mr Pomeroy,' Fielder added.

Adrian couldn't help thinking that for some reason Fielder hadn't finished his sentence. Perhaps, he now realised, Fielder wanted Adrian to finish it himself.

★

Tam pushed past him into the house, going straight for his bedroom. At least the boy was happy to be home.

'You've still got school, don't forget,' Adrian said.

'But I'm already late,' Tam called.

'So? Doesn't mean you can't learn something today.'

Noo trailed behind. She'd refused Adrian's help bringing in the suitcases, asking that he just hurry up and unlock the door for Tam. He obeyed. He held the flyscreen open as she went inside and looked about – what she thought she'd find he had no idea – and went to their bedroom to unpack. She then took Tam to school and didn't come back for a while. He assumed she was getting groceries.

Earlier, when he'd arrived at his parents' place to tell them the good news, to hopefully drive his little family back home, together, his mother hugged him and said, 'See, I told you sense would prevail.' Noo hugged him also, kissed his cheek and said she'd get their things. But it was offhand affection – neither sympathy nor capitulation. It was more like an allowance. Tam was watching television and eating biscuits. Adrian walked over, roughed up his hair and told him the holiday at Grandma's was over. No one said a word about the night before, and Noel and the others were already back at their hotel. Adrian wondered when he'd hear from them.

The rest of the day followed that trend – Noo had possibly the coldest shoulder of any woman alive, and she inflicted it with perfect restraint.

Walking on eggshells was the cliché, and even though he despised clichés, it fitted. A calcified fragility had set in, one they both recognised and dared not stomp on. He tried to get her to sit down and talk but it didn't work – she got busy doing busy things. When he made her a cup of tea she let it go tepid. When he began to speak she left the room. Later, he heard her vomiting. He tapped on the toilet door but she went quiet, coming out long after he'd walked away.

Until that moment he hadn't realised the true impact the allegations had wreaked on her. On her trust in him. On the fortitude of her love, maybe. And through her actions on this day she was making him realise his selfishness – and selfish he had been, he recognised, for too long. How he could restitch the seams of their relationship he had no idea. Perhaps Noo would show him the way. Perhaps their relationship would now operate on her terms.

NGUYET

Nguyet was well aware that white men often thought of Vietnamese women as subservient, but she knew herself to be otherwise. Instead, Nguyet believed in her own tenacity and endurance, and her ability to exercise charm.

Her *mẹ* had taught her about charm and grace from a young age. Charm, her mother had instructed, was the use of complicity and force. Her mother said this many times over the years, perhaps to herself more than to her daughter, and young Nguyet had often wondered if it were some form of mantra to be used in moments of doubt. Doubt in her marriage, her custom – in her being an effective woman, maybe. But Nguyet no longer had to wonder about that because, from her own experience, within her own marriage and her own struggle to hold on to her custom while living in a foreign land, she knew it to be true. There was, after all, so much to doubt that complicity regularly outweighed force, and the negotiation of marriage became a negotiation about how much she could tolerate – and tolerate in silence. *I am being complicit, and force will one day come,* she sometimes told herself. *That balance is the basis of happiness.*

Nguyet thought of these things as she waited for her name to be called. She looked around at the other people, and could hear the two receptionists talking behind the counter. All women. Women waiting for men.

She looked down at her lap and thumbed open her purse. Inside was a wedding photo. *Sự mỉa mai.* There were many ironies to observe in life, but perhaps the greatest was that Nguyet had used her mother's mantras against her in order to justify marrying Adrian. Adrian Pomeroy – the white man, the tourist.

'Such an inauspicious union,' her mother had said at the *an hoi*, the day Adrian arrived, the day before the wedding ceremony, placing not only her own belief but her daughter's future in the Chinese zodiac. 'He is monkey, you are tiger.'

Nguyet knew this wasn't the worst union, but it was said to be characterised by continual disagreement. She put her mother's criticism down to her caution about Adrian being a white man. He did look odd, Nguyet admitted, sweating in his black dinner suit, unable to handle Vietnam's heat, not understanding much of what was going on around him, asking her to translate, to decode the cultural significance of objects and gestures, her having to take the lead. To her mother, none of this was right. And yet she let her daughter have her way. That day, her mother chose complicity.

Adrian came from the airport in a taxi, and her family greeted him with much smiling and nodding and shaking of hands, then brought him inside to the table, which was laid out with dishes of catfish and prawn and vegetables and rice. Her family wasn't at all wealthy – the apartment was small, with two bedrooms for the six of them, the kitchenette and dinner table and bath all in one room, their clothes hung to dry over the bathtub – but they weren't impoverished, as many of Nguyet's friends were.

Hai was especially poor. She had been there when Nguyet first started talking to Adrian online – giggling, asking if Adrian had a brother or friend who would want a Vietnamese girl. Hai had shared in Nguyet's growing affection for Adrian and his chatroom messages. She had witnessed what could only be called Nguyet's quick addiction to the contact, and encouraged her to do the first online video call. She had helped Nguyet choose an outfit to wear, how best to do her hair. But when Nguyet started going to the internet cafe every day to video chat, Hai stopped coming along, and eventually they ceased talking. Nguyet knew it was jealousy, but felt she had no reason to apologise. She felt much the same when it came to family.

As they sat around the table and talked and ate, her family called Adrian *du khách*, the tourist. Nguyet had laughed along with them, although ashamed that Adrian was here in her cluttered home, partaking of the food as well as the indignities of the room. She watched him closely, and wondered if he was normally so red-faced, or if it was the humidity, or maybe the heat in the food. Perhaps it was nerves. A rash rose around his collar, up the side of his neck. She wanted to reach out and touch the skin there, but knew not to – they had not yet touched at all. Somehow they had failed to do so when he arrived, such was the commotion around making sure he met her family in the proper way, they who would become his family the next day, if all went well. Then he was bustled inside by her *bố* and sat at the table. Her younger brother and sisters wanted to sit with Adrian, but her *mẹ* made sure Nguyet was seated beside him.

Their first touch was at the elbow, a rub of the skin which made her strangely conscious of her arm – how she held it, how she could wield it to steal yet another touch, soon getting what she wanted. That seemed to grant him permission to be bolder than her, and he casually dropped his hand beneath the table to place it on her thigh – only for seconds, but long enough to make her hold her breath, as though the gesture tied strings to the ends of his fingers that were directly joined to her heart.

When she regained her breath, she looked up and met her mother's cautious eyes as the old woman spooned more food onto Adrian's plate and implored, '*Ăn ăn người gầy.*'

Her little brother said, 'Thin man, thin man,' in his best English and pulled at Adrian's other elbow.

After the meal, the women cleaned and the men sat outside at a table overlooking the street and introduced Adrian to rice wine, passing around a communal shot glass. That evening her uncle gave Adrian a decorative arrangement of betel nuts in a red dish, which he was to present to her parents, requesting permission to marry. Her *mẹ* and *bố* received the dish with gratitude, and then invited Adrian to sit with them on the floor and chew the nuts with lime paste, her *mẹ*'s hands showing willingness while her eyes still refused.

This reticence continued the next day, even as Nguyet stood in her *áo dài* of red silk, the red *khan đóng* like a halo; even as her brothers and sisters lined up outside the house and held out red lacquered boxes of cakes, wine, betel nuts and roasted pig, offerings draped in red silk, in lieu of Adrian's family. And reticence still as Nguyet and Adrian knelt at the family altar, her mother and father lighting candles, before the couple turned to her parents' feet and accepted two envelopes of money.

All these things, she could see, overwhelmed Adrian, who said nothing, and she thought him small right then, sweltering in the suit he'd hired from a shop in Australia. Australia – a place she'd heard about from friends, even though none had ever been there. She knew Adrian lived in Sydney, so she had read as much about the city as she could find online, although she knew this would mean little once she left Vietnam and landed on foreign soil. As she looked at Adrian, pink-fleshed like a pig, Nguyet understood that he was gaining a family but she was losing her country. She was happy here, there was no denying, but there was also no denying the opportunity Australia offered. From that day on, their relationship would be one of give and take, of gain and loss, of force and complicity. Tiger and monkey.

After the ceremony a neighbour brought her fat baby boy to the apartment and placed him on Nguyet's bed to improve her chances of having a son, her mother insisting that to be happy she must have many children, especially boys. Years later, Nguyet sent the neighbour a card and photo of Tam, thanking her for this luck.

And now here she was, waiting. This time, she had found a way to use force.

★

Her decision to pursue a second child regardless of Adrian's wishes came earlier in the year. They'd been arguing over whether or not to have another baby for over four years. She'd begun the conversation with a soft strategy, saying that because Tam had grown less dependent, perhaps they could start thinking about a second child. But Adrian parried, arguing that Tam's independence gave them more opportunities to do things as a family, and that a new baby would be a step backwards in this regard. She said that Tam had begun asking for a brother or sister to play with, but Adrian replied that they could play with him and teach him good things through play, or that he could go to daycare and Nguyet could find a better job and contribute more to the finances. This had stung her.

Nguyet wasn't one to argue. She never raised her voice and preferred to communicate emotion through gesture, yet Adrian had aggravated her. Her final appeal was that she had grown up in a large family: family meant everything in her culture. Each time she phoned her family her mother asked what was wrong, why she wasn't having more babies, so Nguyet called them less and less, out of shame.

When Nguyet told Adrian that she would only consider a trip back to Vietnam if she had another child in her arms, he had held out his hands in protest and said that he loved his small family very much, but that didn't mean he shared her desire to keep growing it.

At that, she turned her shoulder so she did not have to look at him.

'Tam is enough,' he had said. 'Tam is everything.'

And so he was. But Nguyet knew that everything could also be found in another – that love would not be halved, but doubled.

This went on for several years, becoming the topic of no conversation and yet somehow every conversation. It was present even in the most trivial things, the things that husbands and wives must say to each other on a daily basis so the household can function. All their conversations were inflected with Nguyet's discontent – her embarrassment at the rejection, at the selfishness of her husband, at her fantastical excuses when she spoke to her mother on the phone and the inevitable question was asked. She turned her shoulder to him more and more, and eventually they made love less and less. It was his only way to reduce the chances of pregnancy, she felt, and in her more cynical moments she wondered whether he suspected her of popping her contraceptive pills into the drain instead of her mouth. When she thought about this too much her gut cramped and she would vomit. She knew his fear each time this happened, worrying that it was a symptom of the other thing, the unspoken thing, the unreasonable and unconvincing thing. But no. It was only her anxiety over wanting that thing.

Why he did not share her want confounded her. She knew the reason couldn't be practical: they could afford another child, both financially and in the love they had left in them. Especially if what they had given Tam was any indication – and what Tam had given them. Adrian was a good father, an involved father, an intelligent man with a soft voice and plenty of heart and time to offer those he cared for, cared about. He wasn't domineering. He never raised his hand, and only sometimes his voice, when need dictated. So his aversion made no sense.

A reason must exist, she told herself, and she began asking him about work stresses, about whether he should consider other options. He denied anything but the usual difficulties of trying to teach teenage boys something about how to express themselves, about being persuasive, about life. Another form of employment wasn't an option, he said: he'd been working hard at establishing his career as a teacher and wasn't about to let that go, especially for no good reason, just a bit of stress in the workplace. Stress she wouldn't and couldn't understand, he told her – which was a blunt thing to say, and unlike him.

Around this time she noticed his quietness, and there was something else in him that had also changed. Something she could not identify, let alone confront. She suspected that whatever was holding their family back was coming to some kind of crisis point. And maybe – she hoped, prayed – maybe even a resolution.

During the months that followed she kept a closer eye on Adrian and his movements. She took advantage of the times he invited Rafiq, Amy and their kids to dinner, listening to their conversations, reading between the lines, asking Amy elliptical questions to see whether Rafiq had mentioned Adrian at home, watching Adrian interacting with their sons. Nguyet became an expert listener. She suppressed the urge to be heard and instead found a certain power through observation. Some assumed her English wasn't good, and this only strengthened her. It granted her knowledge. And with this knowledge she could position herself in social circumstances to gain a surreptitious hand. Not that she wielded this hand – the power was in knowing what she perceived, what she knew.

One night, Adrian slipped. He'd been in the study, preparing a lesson on the computer, and when he'd had enough he went and got into the shower, complaining of an aching neck. Nguyet went into the study and saw that he'd left his email open. She scrolled through it, fully aware of the breach but justified in her thinking. Almost all of it was mundane – administration, student queries about assignments and grades. But then she came across someone calling themselves *godhand*. This person had emailed three times with no message, but each time there was an attachment. She opened these, beginning with the first. They were stories.

She didn't know what they signified – what they meant to Adrian, why they'd been sent or what they revealed about her husband – but it was clear that Adrian was a character in the stories. One even described her and Tam, the house. All this was deeply disturbing. All this gave her cause to say something, to ask questions, to make accusations, to shout out the resentment she now felt towards him, but she chose not to. Not right then, anyway.

She chose instead to remain silent, to watch, to exercise charm – complicity and force. She didn't know what her husband had done, but she knew it was something foolish. Nguyet would not be foolish. And so she waited.

And waited.

And then the allegations were made, and then the police knocked and took Adrian away, allowing her time to swear out loud, to cry, and then to centre herself again and regain her sense of determination. She packed two suitcases and collected Tam from school, and then she waited again, this time for Adrian to arrive home, so he could see her walk away. Perhaps that might provoke him into opening up, to finally lay bare his problems. She hoped, too, that one day soon he would provide a reason for her to come back home. Until then, she would wait.

★

Thumbing the wedding photo in her purse, Nguyet knew that waiting was the right thing to do. She still felt the strings attached to her heart, and that those strings were tied to the hands of a good man, a decent man, her husband, Adrian Pomeroy. In this she trusted.

A door opened and a male doctor came from his consulting

room. He leant over the reception counter and was handed a folder – a folder Nguyet knew held antenatal ultrasound images. A folder that held black and white etchings of a truth, like black words on white paper, and determined the terms of a new life – a life that looked forward, not backward.

The doctor turned to face the waiting room. 'Mrs Pomeroy?' he said.

She closed her purse, stood and smiled.

'I am Nguyet.'

FIVE

NOEL

Noel knew he was too close to everything, and that everything was too close. This impossible city, this impossible family. To call it suffocation would be downplaying what he felt right then, right there in the hotel room with Wendy packing her shit. He was getting his wish. But he also felt pissed that she and the girls were hitting the road to the nation's capital, especially in the hire car.

'So? Get a-fucking-nother car,' Wendy said.

He was standing at the window, looking first out at the Parra hubbub below, then at her and the suitcase on the floor, then out again. He'd tried opening the window but it was sealed. The only air coming in was ducted and cold. Like a fridge. Like a fucking tomb. Just like his marriage. Noel smirked at the thought and shook his head.

Wendy looked at him as she folded a shirt into the case, but didn't say anything. Always so fucking neat with her packing – it gave him the shits how immaculate she was sometimes. *Your wife's a real trooper, mate. She's such a catch. Such a trophy. She's immaculate.* Simmo had wanted her bad from day dot, and now Noel regretted not letting him have her. At least then Noel could've basked in the glory of Simmo's dumbstruck face when he rocked up at the station with the full knowledge that Wendy could also be a right cunt.

She refused to say anything about smoking dope with Adrian the night before. Silence as self-defence – that old trick. He knew it well, so he decided to flex his interrogation muscles. 'Weren't you guys in Mum's car?'

No reply.

'He mustn't have had the gear on him, then, so where'd he get it from?'

Nothing.

'Did you drive back to his house or did you meet up with some sleazy dealer?'

Still nothing.

He laughed. 'You've always had a thing for Adrian. Probably sucked him off in the driver's seat.'

'Excuse me?'

Right on the money.

Wendy went on. 'Lower your voice – you know the kids are just next door, and they shouldn't have to hear that crap coming out of your mouth right now.'

'What, the princess and the tranny?'

Wendy's expression showed the explosions going off within the confines of her dim little head, so he decided to keep pushing. It was the only way he felt like he was getting a victory. Push her to spill her guts and feel the bite of guilt – that bitch of a thing he knew so well. He'd come to consider it his muse, the guiding hand behind each of his actions and inactions. Guilt was pressure. Guilt was power. Guilt was Noel's motivation, but it was also his release. Was it like pressing a scar? Nup. More like fingering an open wound. It was time others understood that too – the full force of culpability come home to roost. His wife was simply the first in line.

'So did you suck him off or what?'

'Did *you*?' Wendy said.

'What the fuck's that supposed to mean?'

He knew exactly what that meant.

Wendy was the one shaking her head this time. 'Noel, you sometimes forget the things you say.'

He recalled no such conversation, but it didn't matter – he didn't want a bar of it. 'I bet you did. I bet you smoked a joint and got all cosy in the car and that's why you're taking off – because you can't handle it. You're so transparent.'

'We're leaving because Adrian doesn't need us to be here. Especially with the case being dropped. And we're leaving because—'

'The case isn't dropped, only the allegations. Get it right.'

'And we're leaving because we've all had enough of your bullshit to last us another week without you. At the very least.'

'Rightio.' He stood beside the suitcase, arms crossed. 'At the very least, hey. What's that supposed to mean?'

If he pushed hard enough, he knew, she'd make the choice he could never make himself, and not because he was emotionally dependent on them but because his deceit depended on everything else staying normal. He'd replaced his own family with a constructed one; he'd taken Wendy to Perth to free himself of his dependencies, but he'd ended up creating another. But he knew now that his pathway to destruction had progressed beyond rescue; that he no longer needed his family, and they didn't need him.

'You know what that means, Noel. You're intelligent enough to work that one out for yourself. You don't need me to mother you anymore, and I sure as shit don't need to carry your baggage anymore.'

Good, he thought. *Let's go for broke.* 'You're such a fucking teenager,' he said.

She stopped zipping up the suitcase to laugh, incredulous. '*I'm* the teenager? Do you know how ridiculous that is? While you've been doing your little disappearing act – for quite some time now, I might add – I've been the responsible one, looking after the finances, raising our children—'

Noel just had to smile at that one.

'—and even though I have no idea where you go or what you get up to, I know that deep down you're still just a teenage boy, acting out, playing for sympathy, knowing that I'll be there to clean up after you and tuck you into bed. It's sad. It's pathetic. It's time you grew some real fucking substance, Noel. Your kids need it and I need it, so maybe some time away will force you to mop up after yourself and learn some responsibility.'

Wendy pulled the case up onto its wheels, then yanked out the handle and made her way to the door. Noel rushed over just as she opened it, slamming it shut with his left palm. He held his right fist to her face. She winced. He was so close he could smell coffee on her breath, the complimentary shower gel on her skin. He longed to kiss her.

He lowered his fist. 'We're all guilty, Wendy,' he said. 'We all have something to be sorry for.'

She rolled her eyes and put her hand on the handle. 'Go to hell,' she said, then she pulled open the door and closed it behind.

A moment later he heard her talking to Grace and Riley in the room next door.

I'm already there, he thought.

Within minutes they and all their voices were gone.

*

Noel was on a roll so he figured he'd just go with it, even if it took him to perilous places.

He laced his shoes and headed out. First he organised another car, grabbing a taxi to a rental depot, doing the paperwork and eventually making his way back to the hotel via a bottle shop. On his way past the front desk he asked the staff for some blank paper and a pen, which he took with his whisky up to his room.

He removed his shoes, then poured a drink and put it on the floor next to the bed. He cleared the lamp and clock radio from the bedside table and shifted it in front of him, put the blank paper and pen on top, then reached again for his drink, draining the glass. He got up and poured another, this time right to the rim. He sipped, then replaced it on the floor and looked at the white sheet of paper.

He calmed. He breathed. He composed himself as best he could.

It wasn't as though he didn't know what to write. He'd had years to come up with the right words. He'd composed this letter a thousand times over – sometimes while taking out grubs, sometimes after sex, often while doing nothing much at all. And always at a burn. That was the best time, the time he came closest to knowing the words it'd take to redress what he'd done. He'd wanted to start the conversation a long way back but hadn't known how. Picking up the phone, calling Adrian to say it was about time they had a talk – it was a simple enough action, but that didn't indicate how difficult it truly was.

But in his current state of mind Noel thought, *Fuck it.* The way he saw it, Adrian had been screwed over recently, and Noel had a distinct feeling it had something to do with what he himself had done all those years ago. That somehow those actions had been seduced back to life – into both their lives. Noel had watched Adrian with Tam and Nguyet and admired him for what he'd made for himself. And now that Adrian was probably in the clear, he didn't need his big brother around to look out for him, nor did he need manifestations of the past fucking things up for him again.

No. It was time for the end. Or what he hoped would become the end. He had no idea how Adrian would react, but tried not to think about that. Right then, it was all about getting the words down. It was about getting that ghost and pinning it to the page, each pen stroke stabbing that bastard of a thing right in the heart.

And so Noel wrote …

And afterwards, he drank. He drank so deep and long that for a few hours he forgot.

*

The next morning Noel got up and got going. He drove to Adrian's place, parking several houses down and on the opposite side of the road. He watched the house for movement.

Nguyet and Tam came out first, getting into the car, ready for the school run. The car pulled out of the driveway and left in the other direction. Noel then had to wait for Adrian. He knew Adrian had no car, but he hoped he might step out for some reason, during which time he'd have the chance to get inside the house.

Failing that, he'd have to use a different method, a more direct one, perhaps knocking on the door and going inside for a chat – two brothers catching up. At least there was stuff to tell him, with Wendy and the girls taking off for Canberra, and he could always ask how things were going with the case. Finding conversation points would be easy, but he didn't know if he had the stomach for that. Not now. Not with what he'd written and what he was set on delivering. Because that had to happen, one way or the other, before he came to regret it. And that moment would inevitably arrive.

Midmorning, Adrian came out the front door and headed along the footpath, in the direction of Noel and the hire car. Noel sank low in the seat and was thankful the car wasn't recognisably his, staying down until Adrian had passed – stretching his legs, probably. Once he was well out of sight, Noel got out of the car and got to work.

★

This was an invasion – Noel knew that – even though his intent wasn't to take but to give.

Gaining access was fairly straightforward. He slipped down the side of the house and checked if any windows had been left open or unlocked – nothing. There was a shed in the back yard, containing a lawn mower and some tools. He picked up a decent screwdriver and hammer from a shelf, then walked to the laundry window. The screwdriver's flat head wedged neatly between the window frame and sliding panel, so he only had to tap it with the hammer a few times before the lock jumped the latch. The window slid open. How simple it was to be a burglar, it struck him: all it really took was common sense, and a complete lack of empathy for the people you were fucking over.

Noel didn't muck about. Experience told him that the people who get busted doing this kind of thing were the ones who lingered too long. He only had to find a place to put the letter – somewhere Adrian's wife and kid wouldn't find it first.

He walked the rooms and went into the study. He opened a desk drawer and placed the letter down, but then thought again. He had no idea how long it would take Adrian to find it there – and there was a good chance Nguyet might open the drawer first. No, he had to be smarter than that. He walked into their bedroom and saw the book on the bedside table. A book – of course. That was ideal.

He let the book fall open in his hands and slipped the folded pages inside. He closed the book, put it back on the table and looked around the bedroom one last time to reinforce his decision. He then went and shut the laundry window, unlatched the lock on the back door and shut it behind him. After putting the tools back in the shed, he made his way back to the street and the hire car.

During the drive to the hotel Noel began to shiver. He tried to light a ciggie but couldn't. He hit the steering wheel with the meat of his palm. *Grow some balls, you pussy*, he told himself, but before long he had to pull over on a service road. He got out, bent and vomited into the gutter.

'Noel,' he said aloud, standing and wiping his mouth, 'you're losing it, buddy.'

ADRIAN

If something could be said to definitively deny the past, to wipe clean what one thinks is real, and instead reveal it to be a false memory, part of childhood make-believe – what then? What if this were the only crime to be found guilty of, and all others were wrongly accused? What if the event which Adrian Pomeroy believed formed the foundation of his identity were obliterated? Who would he become? He would still be Adrian Pomeroy the husband, father, son, brother – he would still be that person because that is who he is to others. But what about who he is to himself? Would his own construction of himself be altered somehow if someone were to outright deny what he had always believed to be the substance, the grist, of his past? Their past?

And what if that past were to be undeniably confirmed? What then?

Adrian has heard people say they don't understand why the abused are reluctant to speak out long after the event. Perhaps because talking about it might just be its undoing, and the undoing of you. Memory made unreal, or memory made real – it's a lose-lose situation.

While Adrian has never asked to have done to him what was done, he would not now want it to be taken back. He concedes that this is a strange certitude, but it is a certitude nonetheless.

★

Adrian found the letter tucked into the pages of *The Stories of John Cheever*.

It was late. He was in bed with the lamp on when he reached over, picked up the book and saw paper wedged inside. His initial thought was of Alex – that Alex had made contact, that he'd penned another story, only his delivery method had changed, for obvious reasons. But anyway, it would confirm that Alex still wanted him – was still watching him, even, the proof being that he'd somehow gained access to the house while no one was home. But then the thought crossed his mind that perhaps he assumed incorrectly: that this was a different kind of story altogether – a hateful story, a story of regret. Perhaps this was the severing of what they'd held between them, the cutting of a cord that was tenuous in any case. One final story to undo what had been done. A goodbye fable.

He looked across at Nguyet lying on her side, facing away from him. There'd been no progress with her, with them; it would take time and a gentle rhythm to return them to each other's arms. Adrian should have shown her, of course – should have told her from the very beginning – but full disclosure requires a careful tongue, and well-timed execution.

He looked back at the book and butterflied it open to see the letter, and instantly knew this wasn't the hand of Alex. No, *godhand* was not at work here. This was something else entirely. And upon seeing his brother's handwriting – that clumsy scrawl he could recognise anywhere – a precise knowledge came over him about why the letter was here at all: why Noel would choose to write to him, such an uncharacteristic thing for him to do.

There could be only one reason why, and Adrian was intelligent enough to work it out without reading the letter. In fact, he felt a strange rising of defiance. Noel hadn't changed at all: he was still finding ways to impress himself on Adrian's life, despite his shifting to Perth, despite their carving out separate families and careers and ways of thinking about and acting within their lives. And in that moment he didn't care whatsoever whether Noel was resurrecting their sad and intimate tale just to further underline his ability to control, to dominate his little brother, to exercise force, or whether this was some bizarre apology, that Noel's remorse had slowly built up over the years, and the recent events in Adrian's life had pushed Noel beyond a tipping point, that he finally felt strongly enough and had either the courage or the stupidity enough to come out with it all and face what were now only phantasms, breathing words into those visions of a past to bring them into the light, to make them real, to make them felt all over again. Tangible. As tangible as the folded paper packed into his book.

Fuck him, Adrian thought. *Fuck him and his words, whatever they say.*

But at the same time he was grateful that the letter was there, that he had the letter in his hands – in a book, of all places. It was a gift, after all. Noel had gifted him acknowledgement, and in that acknowledgement – which Adrian had forever wondered, at least from his early teenage years, whether he'd ever receive – Noel had also gifted Adrian a sense of control, of authority. In writing The Apology, Noel had also given authority to Adrian's memories, to his concept of self – as muddled and affected and misguided as that concept sometimes was. Yes. The letter represented a small but magnificent victory – small because it was his and his only, but magnificent because of what it meant for him, Adrian Pomeroy.

And so he didn't read the letter right away. He left it folded into the book's pages. He said to his wife's back that he was too tired to read, and then switched off the lamp so it was dark. Dark enough to curl into his mind and close in on his thoughts.

★

When Adrian read the letter the following morning, he cried. He cried in two ways: as the six-year-old boy he was, and as the thirty-six-year-old man that boy had led into that very moment.

And he was thankful, because now he could begin a new process. Now he could finally let go of the grief of not knowing, and understand the relief of confession.

★

Adrian can still hear his brother's battle cry: 'I will protect you!'

The bush cubby was the place to play attack and defence games. Noel and his mates would go down there with Adrian in tow, the younger brother who always ended up being the hostage while the older boys skirmished through the bush with sticks for guns. Adrian thought it was the best thing to hang out with the older boys and do rough stuff, and he felt a surge of pride at witnessing his brother doing anything to protect him: liberating him from the bindings, cutting the imaginary rope with an imaginary knife, picking him up from the cubby floor and running off into the bush with him to declare victory.

When the boys got tired of imagining they went to the next level, stealing real rope from Connor's dad's garage and a paring knife from Glenda's kitchen drawer. Then the games really began. Adrian could recall with clarity the grit and grain of the cubby floorboards against his face as he lay there hogtied one day, unable to move, watching the bush through the open doorway, waiting for movement, occasionally hearing the snap of a stick as Connor scoped the cubby perimeter, on the lookout for Noel.

And on this day Noel had taken Connor by surprise, jumping from a tree and knocking Connor on the head as he landed. Connor had screamed and stormed off home in tears. Next thing Noel climbed the ladder and stood in the doorway, looking down at Adrian. They could hear Connor crunching up the path and away.

'What happened to Connor?' Adrian said.

'Don't worry about him. He's a sook. Can you move?'

Adrian wriggled. 'Nope. He tied it good this time.'

Noel looked out the window. 'Good.'

And just when Adrian thought Noel was going to untie the rope, he felt Noel's hands around his waist, his fingers in the hemline of his pants, pulling down.

That wasn't the first or last time.

★

Adrian bit the bullet and told Nguyet he had to go see Noel, so he dropped her at work and headed to Parramatta.

As he drove he tried to rehearse what he'd say, but he couldn't think clearly. He felt emotionally stable, but he also felt the familiar heat coming up from the pit of his stomach.

But he figured not knowing exactly what to say might be better – perhaps then they'd just talk like two brothers, without pretence. The more he thought about this, the more he trusted the idea.

He parked out front of the hotel, then went in and asked at the desk for Noel's room number. The receptionist handed over a slip of paper. He thanked her and took the lift up to the right floor. The room was just a couple of doors along. Standing outside, Adrian looked back at the lift, then at the door. He took a deep breath, reminded himself why he was there, and knocked.

No answer.

He waited, then knocked again.

'Noel,' he called, leaning into the door. 'Wendy – are you guys there?' He looked at the slip of paper again to check he had the right room.

He then knocked again, harder this time, with more knocks. It sounded like urgency, desperation. Insistence. He realised all three applied.

'Noel,' he called again, then waited again, before turning away.

He sat in the car while he considered what to do. He still had no phone, but he figured there was a good chance Noel might be at their parents' place. And if not, then at least Glenda might know where he was, or they could try calling his mobile. He started the car and pulled away.

When he arrived, Glenda was watching a movie.

'Have you heard from Noel lately?' Adrian asked her.

Glenda shook her head, said she'd asked him to dinner last night because Wendy and the kids had left him on his own while they went to Canberra, but he had other plans. 'I asked him what kind of plans but he said he had to go. Why?'

Adrian shook his head as if it didn't matter. He looked out the window to the back yard, where his dad, in his old workshop coveralls, was fiddling with an engine part. Adrian hadn't seen him in those coveralls for a long time. A tarp was spread across the lawn and bits of the kit car sat on it.

'Is he finally going to finish that thing?' Adrian asked.

'Who knows? Whatever keeps him from drinking for a while, I say.'

'Yeah,' Adrian said. 'Listen, do you mind if I use the phone?'

He tried Noel's mobile but it went straight to message. He then phoned Wendy. He hadn't spoken to her since the family dinner and the pot, and it occurred to him that maybe Wendy taking off had something to do with all this.

'Wen, is there any chance you've heard from Noel today?'

'No chance,' she said, 'and I think it's better that way, to be honest. A bit of distance can only be a good thing right now.'

'That bad, huh. Is it because of the other night?'

She sighed. 'It's bigger than that, I'm afraid. Why do you want him?'

'Just a bit worried. I think I should talk to him but I can't track him down.'

'Save yourself. I'm sure he'll turn up soon enough. You know what they say — you can't keep a good man down.'

★

Over the following two hours Adrian's anxiety increased, and it began to rub off on his mother. Noel still wasn't answering his mobile, so Adrian called the hotel and asked them to pass on a message when he came back.

Wendy called back to say she still hadn't heard from him,

but that she had checked their banking records and he'd hired a car. She dismissed the suggestion that there was an issue, and said again that Noel had been disappearing like this a lot lately, but he always turned up. She said she'd let Adrian know if she heard from him.

Glenda tried to distract herself in the kitchen, but Adrian heard her mumbling about things turning bad, about how she'd known something was going to happen. As though this unease had triggered some prophecy in his mother.

They mentioned it to Mal but he didn't say anything. Occasionally he'd come into the house and stand there listening – present, but not fully.

After a while Adrian decided to drive back to the hotel, but he knew that was useless – it was more an excuse to keep moving, to keep himself from thinking that the letter wasn't only an apology but something greater, the kind of letter loved ones never want to read. The kind of letter that provides more than one sense of closure.

No luck.

He waited in the hotel foyer for a while, but when he tired of that he returned home and phoned Noel's mobile again. This time he left a message: 'Noel, just wondering where you are. Everyone is. Call me as soon as you get this.'

He went to the bedroom and got the letter out and read it again. He looked for clues to what he dreaded, but found nothing giving that impression.

He called again half an hour later and left another message: 'Noel, I'd really like to talk. I'm sorry about what happened the other night with Wendy, and you shouldn't be angry at her. Anyway … just call me when you get this, okay.'

The phone rang as soon as he hung up, but it was Glenda. She was getting herself fully worked up now. She said she'd called the police but they told her there wasn't much to do at this stage except log the call. She told them Noel was a police officer but that didn't help. 'Then he should know how to find himself,' the officer said.

She asked Adrian what he thought – about what might be wrong, about whether they were overthinking things and there was nothing wrong at all – but Adrian didn't say what he feared. He maintained optimism, casualness even, regardless of his distrust for the words coming from his own mouth. All his thoughts had become edged with a sense of threat.

A third message, a short time later: 'What are you doing, Noel? I mean, seriously – what the fuck?'

After he hung up he looked at the letter in his hands and asked himself where Noel might go. Out of the whole of Sydney, where would Noel go?

And then Adrian realised. No, he knew.

NOEL

After delivering the letter Noel set about getting decently stonkered in the hotel room, doing nothing except watching TV and drinking whisky – until he passed out, he hoped. But it didn't quite go that way. First was a phone call from Glenda, inviting him to dinner, but he put on his best sober voice and tried not to say too much except that he had something on. He thought about phoning Wendy to see how they were getting on, but realised that hearing from him was the last thing she'd want. He'd pretty much done his dash there, he figured.

Soon after, he got to watching a movie he'd heard the name of but never seen. It was about four kids who did a foolish thing and ended up in a youth reform centre for over a year. In that time a guard perceived their weakness and set about exploiting it, getting them to suck his dick and probably some other stuff too. It wasn't shown. The movie then skipped to when the boys were men, and two of them were at a bar for a drink and a meal. Things hadn't been that great in their lives – drugs, violence, prison. One of the men got up to go to the toilet and on the way he saw a guy sitting in a booth, eating. He knew the guy – there was instant recollection, the kind you can't mistake. When he came back to the bar he got his mate to check the guy out and confirm what he'd seen – who they'd seen. They had guns, these two. They walked over and sat opposite the guy, and there was some vague talk and the guy had an attitude because he just wanted to eat his meal. They had to remind him who they were, who he was to them. One of the men held a gun under the table aimed at the guy's crotch. They talked a bit more, telling the guy it was his last meal, so it was a shame to see what he'd ordered. Then the trigger was pulled.

Noel turned it off then. He couldn't bear to see any more.

He screwed the lid back on his bottle and put it aside, then turned off the light and tried to sleep. The room wasn't as black as he was used to at home, and there was traffic noise and occasional shouting from the street below. But these things didn't affect him. If anything, they were welcome distractions, if only he could focus on them, allow them to lull him to sleep. Instead, he could only see the guy's face from the movie – his horror at realising who the two men were, those boys who he'd made to suck and fuck, and what they now appeared as before his death – dressed in black like his death had already occurred, and in mourning for the death of the thing inside them, a death he was responsible for, all those years ago. And even though his hair was longer and he was no longer in his shiny uniform, it was as though no time had passed at all. Their deaths were as fresh as today, and would continue to be fresh tomorrow, until an end could be found – their own ends, each and every one of them. Especially his.

As Noel lay there this horror seared his mind, and although he knew there were no men sitting opposite him with guns and there never would be – Adrian would never have what it took to point any type of weapon at him – he also knew that his letter was an invitation to sit at the table, to talk, to face each other and face off the little death Noel had delivered in their youth. And he didn't know if he could endure that confrontation. Looking down the barrel of what he'd done. Sometimes planned, sometimes just taking advantage of opportunity. But always perpetrated by him.

Yes, this guy's horror was Noel's own horror. But Noel's was worse, because there was no bullet in that movie gun, and that blood wasn't real. The other guy was only acting. Not like what Noel had done. Noel had no such easy way out.

*

He woke the next morning with remarkable clarity of mind.

He showered and dressed, then ate breakfast over a complimentary newspaper in the hotel cafe. He returned to his room, tidied his things, then grabbed his backpack and put the newspaper, bottle of scotch, cigarettes and lighter inside, and finally his hire car keys.

He headed north this time. Kellyville was only a half-hour drive or so, and in the Sydney of his memory Kellyville marked the end of the urban area and the beginning of farmland and scrubby bush tracts, stretching all the way to Windsor. There had to be plenty of places for a burn.

As he drove, he smoked and thought about not much at all. Everything was screwed to the bullshit so there wasn't much use in thinking about anything but the houses and pedestrians he passed, on the side of Sydney he had always liked best. He recognised the streetscapes for the most part, but as he drove further he began to feel dislocated. New estates had erupted from pockets of land, crammed like tins on a supermarket shelf. And it was the same when he got to what he guessed was Kellyville: whole new residential and commercial areas stretched across the landscape, well beyond recognition.

He shook his head but drove on. It had to finish sooner or later – the sprawl couldn't go on forever. Yet the further he drove, the more it seemed that way, so he pulled into a side street and drove through an estate, looking at the gleaming houses, partly because he didn't want to turn around and go back just yet, but also because he hoped he might reach a margin, that somewhere on the other side of this suburban nightmare there might be his burn time. And he did find a place, though it was more like a nature corridor, a strip of bush bordering a creek.

He parked and got out to take a look. Houses were nearby – way closer than for any other burn he'd done – but the road between the bushland and the houses was fairly wide so he figured it would be safe enough. The biggest challenge was not being seen.

He grabbed his backpack and headed along a concrete path, which soon became gravel, then gave way to a dirt track. The creek was dry, and there wasn't much understorey vegetation except for dry grass here and there. None of it would suit. He kept walking until he came across another track. He saw flashes of colour through the trees, meaning he'd just about hit the other side of the corridor. Beyond that was more of the estate. He soon found a section of the creek that was lower, where the trees were thinned out and there was a good bed of long grass – wetter, but dry enough for a decent burn.

He put the backpack on the ground and fished out his cigarettes, lighter and the newspaper. He halved the newspaper and rolled it lengthways, then rolled the other half the same way. These would flare nicely once they caught, and they were dense enough to generate the heat needed to catch the grass. He lit a cigarette and smoked, hunched over the newspaper rolls. He worked out where he'd place them, about two hand-spans apart, deep in the grass yet open enough that they wouldn't be smothered.

But something didn't feel right. None of this resembled his usual process. It felt rushed, unplanned. Too open to risk. He was also leaving evidence all over the place. He stood, shook his head and thought about heading back. But the burn inside was there, beyond doubt. He looked up at the trees as if for an answer, then across the creek bed. Finally he told himself to grow some balls and just get on with the job.

He dragged on the ciggie and knelt down, then glanced up at the track. There he saw a boy, a kid about twelve years old, who'd stopped on the path and was eyeing Noel with a mix of curiosity and suspicion. Noel had a roll of newspaper in his hand and was holding a lighter to it. He didn't move. The kid stared for a moment, like a wild animal assessing the situation, then turned and ran back up the track.

Noel knew he had to get this over and done with. Now.

He lit the first roll and placed it, then did the same with the second. As it caught, he chucked the lighter and his cigarettes in his bag and slung it over his shoulder, standing back to see how the fire was lifting, the heat being created, and how the paper took. Within two minutes it was away, and Noel breathed. He felt more relaxed than he'd been at any time over the past few days, since the first Sydney burn.

He watched the fire take hold as he smoked his ciggie

down to the butt, which he flicked into the grass. Then he heard a man's voice from behind. Noel turned. The kid had returned with his dad.

'Oi!'

Noel took off. He cut a way down the embankment, across the dry creek bed and up the other side, turning only to see the guy giving chase, his kid not far behind. Noel kept a decent pace as he pushed through the scrubby growth, and soon could see light on the other side and then some colour. Within moments he stumbled out onto a grass verge running alongside the road, devoid of cars except for his, parked less than a hundred metres away. Back in the bush he could hear the dad pushing – the snap of sticks and the swish of branches – and the boy shouting for his dad somewhere further in. By the time Noel made it to the car the dad was out on the grass, hands on knees, sucking air, his son just breaking out from the tree line.

The buzz was breathtaking. He'd run down plenty of grubs over the years in the service, but escape was an exhilaration altogether different. As he drove off, laughing and hollering at the windscreen, he understood the appeal of doing a runner, outstripping the chase with the fill of adrenaline. Evasion. Elusion. The cut and run. What a hoot.

After two right turns he was heading south along a street parallel to the bush – he knew this because a thin plume of dirty grey smoke was rising above the houses. He made another turn further south, which put him back on the same road he'd parked on, but the dad and boy were out of sight now. He idled on the road shoulder, waiting for the smoke to take on more shape and substance, but within minutes it eased, turning white. Noel slapped the steering wheel. He watched for a couple more

minutes, then did a U-turn and made his way back into the
estate, searching for a way out.

★

Any satisfaction was short-lived. *So it goes for anything and
everything*, he thought. Because guilt always percolated through,
never more intensely than when he was twelve himself and the
urges took control of him and he took control of Adrian. It was
only ever Adrian, no one else, because Adrian was there and
easy to control. And that satisfaction was unlike anything he'd
experienced in his short life, but the guilt came hard and heavy
in equal measure, with equal force.

He often wondered whether he felt more shame now than
he did back then, after each event, but settled on the idea that
the issue wasn't the amount of shame, but its reach. As a teenager
he was able to tuck the shame beneath bravado or jokes, beneath
his aspiration to be someone better. And a police officer was
that better person – the morally upright figure, community-
minded, selfless. A local hero. But the older he became, the more
difficult it was to conceal the shame. His bravado was called out
as arrogance. His jokes were tasteless, politically incorrect. And
his aspirations led him only into further moral corruption.

That urge. A compulsion that was beyond his ability to
command. It now scorched the landscape because he knew no
other way to get it out. Blotches on the landscape, blistering
the past.

★

Noel knew precisely where to go and what to do there. He
knew Adrian would eventually put one and one together and

end up at the house as well – there were missed calls on his phone from Glenda and Adrian and even Wendy. The search was on. It was what he wanted. Adrian was a smart guy, and Noel himself smart enough to get a plan to work. He congratulated himself with a swig from the bottle, then got out of the car and looked up at the weatherboard beast, still hanging in there after all these years, though the brown trim was gone, now painted Federation green.

He knocked on the door first, as a precaution. The old door. He'd know it anywhere, with the marbled glass window at its centre. He tried the handle, checking its solidity, the size of the deadbolt, which was a piece of piss. He'd busted in plenty of doors like it, and this one gave little resistance, his shoulder colliding with the timber a few times until the bolt shattered through the jamb and the door swung in.

Inside, the house was cold. He didn't remember it this way. It was clear that an Asian family lived here now – the sweet and sour of Asian cooking smells lingered, and there were photos and knick-knacks of a young couple and their boy and girl. They'd renovated – out with the old, in with the new. The hallway carpet had been replaced by tiles, and the walls given a lick of paint. Probably more than one. The scuff marks of his youth were long concealed, but still there beneath – he could feel it, like a tremor between plaster and paintwork. An energy.

He walked into the lounge room. Different curtains, but the windows were just the same. The front room, where they'd played vinyl records as kids, was now a makeshift office. There was no 1970s rug, no veneer sideboard. He went down the hallway to the bathroom and saw that they'd kept the old tub, but everything else had been renovated – surfaces stripped and rejuvenated, replaced. Noel remembered the photos of him and Adrian and Mal in the bath together when Adrian was only a toddler; he must have been about eight, Mal's dark body hair clinging, which he hated and had decided back then he didn't want to inherit. They were the days before. The days of bubble-bath beards and childish entertainments. Hero figures, board games and wrestling on their parents' bed. His old bedroom was now another child's, a girl, with pretty things all neat and pastel that reminded him of Grace's room when she was young. Adrian's room now belonged to a boy, probably just school age, with posters on the walls and toys pretty much just the same.

But none of these superficial changes mattered to Noel. The space was the most important thing, and that had remained the same, even though he was taller and his sense of it had altered. His idea of his place in the world had altered too – at first expanding with possibility, but more recently tapering into something narrow, constrained. Constrained by his relationships, his understanding of himself and what he was not capable of. Somewhere along the line he'd settled for mediocrity. Somewhere between here and Perth he'd allowed himself to think small and act large.

He looked around at the space, the dimensions of doorways and glass panes, the light, and he realised how alien he was here, now. He couldn't work out if the past was a ghost or if he was the ghost haunting the past. Because he was positive the past was still here, built into the structure of the house, into the idea of his youth.

Standing at the doorway of his parents' old room, he could still see his hand pushing the door ajar to see Mal on top of Glenda one humid Sunday afternoon; he swore Mal knew he was there and let him watch anyway. And the time Noel was in his own bedroom and his dad opened the door and laughed at his son standing there naked, bent over, the confused grin as Mal asked what the hell he was doing. Noel had come up with some lame excuse. He remembered looking at Adrian squeezed in behind the door, where he'd pushed him moments before, realising he'd taken things too far and was too close to getting caught.

Noel went out the back door through the kitchen to see the granny flat, but it was no longer there, a large steel and aluminium shed looming in the space where he'd once hung out with his mates before he went off to the academy, where they'd watched movies and tried booze for the first time, where he'd stashed porn in the holes in the plasterboard, which he'd then covered over with posters of rock idols. *Thank Christ that place is no longer here*, he thought. That had been the original place, the site of the first, when he was twelve.

Noel walked back through the house and out onto the front steps. He sat, opened his bag and got out the scotch and his mobile phone. There were three voice messages from Adrian, each one more desperate than the last. It wouldn't be long now. He unscrewed the lid of the bottle and had some, then some more, then he lit a smoke and looked out at the street and waited.

ADRIAN

Pulling up outside the house, he could already see Noel.

The old house, their childhood house. As he walked up the driveway, past Noel's rental car, he looked up at the old place and could sense, even then, the past taking form, as though their stories were etched into the fibrocement walls, the events of their youth strung up from the eaves. It didn't matter that there was fresh paint and a new carport and landscaping – these were superficial amendments, alterations that had no bearing on the house's history. The face was still there, windows for eyes, staring down at him like it was surprised to see him after all these years.

Noel sat on the front step, a bottle of whisky in one hand, more empty than not. Adrian could tell that Noel had been emptying it into himself.

'Little brother,' Noel started, 'welcome home.'

Adrian stopped well short of the steps. 'Noel, what are you doing here? This is someone's house.'

'Exactly, bro, this is our house,' he said, pointing at Adrian and then at his own chest. The drink was well and truly through him. 'This'll always be our place.'

Adrian looked up at the front door. It was open. There was debris on the floor – chipped paint and timber shards. 'Noel—'

'I don't give a flying fuck about who lives here now, because we've got some shit to settle once and for all.'

'Noel, this is piss talk. Come back to my place and we can sort out everything there.'

Noel smiled, nodding. 'So you got my mail, eh?'

Adrian took The Apology from his pocket. 'Yeah, but listen—'

'No, you listen to me, okay, because I wrote that letter and I brought us back and I couldn't care less about the people who live here now, because they aren't here and we are. And anything we've got to say about that' – he shook the bottle at the letter – 'has to be said at this house.'

Noel then swigged from the bottle.

Adrian looked up at the house, at its angles framed by blue sky. They'd kept the big tree out the front – he was glad about that. He wondered what else about the place had remained. Standing there, he felt the house freshly in his blood, its roots set deep inside his marrow. But it wasn't their place to colonise with a discussion about the past.

'Noel, you're not thinking about anyone but yourself.'

'That's bullshit. I was actually thinking about you when I came here, when I wrote that thing.'

'I didn't ask for it, Noel. I didn't ask to start this or end this or whatever it's supposed to be. Why now, anyway? Why are you doing this?'

Noel shook his head, laughing. 'Little bro, I started this a long time ago. Who do you think put a hole in Connor's pool all those years back when we were teenagers? I snuck out one night and put a knife through the wall and ripped the side open. I had to laugh when all the water came pissing out. Would've loved to see their faces when they woke up to a flooded yard.'

Adrian remembered hearing about that. He had never made the connection.

'And remember how the bush cubby got trashed? I did that. Do you get it now? This started a long, long time ago and I've been thinking about it ever since. Shit like that doesn't just go away.'

'I know,' Adrian said quietly. Hearing all this made him light-headed, as though he were entering some form of shock. Noel was undermining his conception of their past, as well as any sense he had of his brother as a good person.

'And the stupid thing is that, now we're here, I can't make up my mind about what to do.'

Adrian understood. Today had always been on the cards — inevitable, even — but now, in the middle of it, they were losing touch with what this was all about, let alone what they should do. Perhaps, as he'd long thought, there was nothing to be done. Simple as that. There was no use arguing over detail, no use in apologies. Sure, Noel was to blame because the actions were his, but should either of them really feel guilty? Adrian didn't want to erase the past. This was not about erasure — it was about ownership. Owning truths. Coming to terms with the emotions attached to certain acts. Learning to move forward, to move on. God, it sounded like a cliché, but it was true.

And despite it all — despite how appalling his brother had been, and still could be — Adrian loved him enough to want something better for him. Adrian understood just how low his brother's mental state had plummeted — and with what

Wendy had said, perhaps the acts against Adrian were the least concerning. He wondered if Noel could fall even further.

Looking at him on the steps of the old house, steeped in the past, the past steeped in him, Adrian feared that yes, Noel was capable of sinking to deeper levels. Adrian knew when his brother meant what he said, and settling this once and for all would only be possible through further actions. Noel Pomeroy was a self-made man, and one capable of graver acts than he'd shown so far. What this might entail, though, Adrian had no idea. He only knew he had to do something, say something.

Adrian crouched so that he was level with his brother.

'Noel.' Noel wouldn't look directly at him. 'I forgive you.'

Noel said nothing.

'If that's what it takes for this to be over with, then I forgive you.'

'Shit happens, eh?' Noel said.

'Shit happens.'

'Simple as that?'

'Simple as that. It was thirty years ago, for Christ's sake.'

Noel swigged again, then placed the bottle beside him on the step and stood. 'Nah,' he said.

Adrian stood too. 'No what?'

'It's not that simple. Not for me.'

'Fucking hell, come on, Noel.'

Noel looked him straight in the eye now. 'Hit me,' he said.

'What?'

'You heard.'

'I'm not going to hit you.'

'Come on, pussy. Just fucken hit me – you hit that prick from next door when we were kids. I know what you're capable of.'

'I'm not hitting you.'

Noel stepped forward and shoved Adrian in the chest with both hands. Adrian staggered backwards into a garden bed.

Noel raised his voice. 'Come on, hit me! I know you want to, so just fucking do it!' Noel stood over him, pumping himself up.

Adrian got back up and came eye to eye with his brother. He wouldn't back down from his pacifism. 'I forgive you,' he said again, calmly. 'I'm not out for revenge – that's not what I'm about.'

Noel was monstrous. Noel was rage.

Adrian didn't care. He continued. 'I've had enough and I'm going home. You should do the same – go back to the hotel.' He looked squarely at the house. 'There's nothing left for us here,' he said finally.

As he turned back towards Noel, he glimpsed a flash of movement, then felt Noel's fist smashing into his nose, splitting the skin again, cracking the bone again, and for a moment Adrian caught sight of his own face from outside himself, witness to the blood and disbelief as he reeled into the garden bed, his head finding ground, losing consciousness.

NOEL

Noel looked at Adrian sprawled in the garden, his bloody nose smeared across his face, out like a light. Next to him was the letter, which he'd dropped as he fell. Noel could still feel Adrian's face on his knuckles. He shook his head and called himself a fuckwit for bashing his little brother; it was a knee-jerk reaction, a moment of panic. He definitely hadn't meant to knock Adrian unconscious. He only wanted to rile him up enough that he would lash out and punch him like he'd done to that neighbour kid, and maybe even unleash what Noel knew must have been boiling inside him for all these years.

Noel bent and picked up the letter. He unfolded it and skimmed over what he'd written the day before. He had to do something about this – he couldn't have it out there, floating around. There was no telling what Adrian would do with it, who he might give it to, who might read those words. Get rid of the letter. Rip it to shreds.

Fuck.

He turned and picked up his whisky, drank some more. He looked at the bottle and then up at the house, and came to the conclusion that he himself was the only fucked-up one here. Adrian had found peace in his own way. Noel always thought it was a secret pact between the two of them – a brutal and sick one, but a pact nevertheless. Now, the thought that Adrian had bowed out was difficult to handle, if only for what it said about his own failings, his own troubled mind. He set about making it otherwise.

Noel went back into the house, shut the broken door as best he could, then pushed a hefty sofa from the lounge room against it as a barricade. He went into the kitchen, screwed up the letter as hard as he could and threw it into the sink. He splashed some of his booze onto the paper, took the lighter from his pocket and lit the thing, then stood back to watch it go. Black smoke came swirling up.

He watched the blaze, felt the heat rise over his face, traces of the past going with it, his words blackening to ash, curling and shedding. Such perfect intensity, feeling the high of being in control, finally, he believed.

Noel stepped back and upended what was left of the booze into his mouth. The room swayed. He sat on the floor and rested against a cupboard door. Exhausted, giddy. Delirious. At the end of something immense he never thought containable. But he'd found a way. For now at least. There would be other stuff to deal with later, but that didn't matter right then. He felt so far from everything familiar, yet so close to himself.

Yellow flickered somewhere higher beside him, the sound of fire like fury embodied, the sound of self-loathing quenched. Somewhere down the hallway a smoke alarm wailed, but Noel eased his back onto the kitchen floor, from where he could look up at the black smoke rippling across the ceiling, creeping down the walls, his past both shrouded and aglow. His adult life had been a slow and sure self-annihilation, but this … in the delirium of now, this was Noel Pomeroy's resurrection. The final burn.

If only Adrian was here to witness it.

ADRIAN

Adrian was brought back to consciousness by the wail of a smoke alarm. He lifted his head from foliage and the centre of his face pulsated. He brought his hands to his nose but didn't touch. There was blood around his mouth, beneath his lips, slicking his teeth. He ran his tongue across his teeth and lips, swallowed, then put his head back down. The alarm continued to bleep for a few moments, before at last registering in his psyche. So did everything else – where he was, what brought him here, drunken Noel and his fist.

The alarm was coming from the house. *Shit – Noel.*

Adrian peeled himself out of the garden bed, went up the steps and pushed on the door. He could see the lock was shattered and the door gave in a little but he couldn't open it. He went to the nearest window, the lounge room, and cupped his hands against the glass to look inside: there was a sofa stuck halfway into the hallway. He turned and grabbed a decent-sized rock from the garden bed and threw it at the window, shattering the glass into wedges. He took off one of his shoes and used it to clear the glass from the frame and sill, then hoisted himself onto it, throwing one leg inside and then the other. His face stung like all hell but he ignored it. He was in.

Smoke hung like haze. He couldn't smell it but could taste it. He bent and looked down the hallway to where it was billowing from the old kitchen, rippling in ropey black currents. Beneath the alarm he could hear the fire, the sound of consumption, of the kitchen coming to pieces.

'Noel!'

No response. He peered out the window but couldn't see his brother, only the rental car in the driveway. Adrian looked back down the hallway. He lifted his shirt collar over his mouth and breathed through it, then crouched lower and moved towards the kitchen.

The closer he edged, the less he could see and breathe. Around halfway he dropped to his stomach and crawled the rest of the length to the kitchen doorway, holding his breath, squinting from the burn, and there he saw Noel face-down on the kitchen floor. Above and behind his body the fire tore at the walls and had opened the ceiling.

The window exploded, casting glass across the kitchen. Smoke released into the sky but the fire blazed higher and harder with the oxygen let in. Adrian reached out and grabbed Noel's arm and heaved him across the tiles to the doorway, inching the dead weight of his brother's body closer, stopping to cough and breathe through his shirt. Eventually he got Noel to the hallway. Adrian then got to his knees and dragged Noel to the front door.

Although the smoke hung lower now, he managed to push the sofa from the door. He turned to his brother, hooked his hands under his armpits and dragged him from the house, gasping down the steps, into clean air, finally. He took Noel onto the grass. Exhausted and wheezing, Adrian sat over his brother and began resuscitation, grateful for the training the school made him do every few years – even for the evacuation tests, which always devolved and made the students manic from the break in routine, the break from curriculum, from classroom tedium. These were the thoughts Adrian had while he pumped Noel's sternum to a measured count, his own blood on his brother's face from where he breathed into his mouth, wincing from the pain of his nose each time but the pain not something to even consider.

He didn't question whether he was doing the right thing – whether Noel wanted Adrian to bring him back from his death. Noel had made a choice, Adrian had intervened. Nor did he think about The Apology, or whether he forgave his brother, because he had already forgiven him long ago. Forgetting was an impossibility, as long as he remained in his own skin, but forgiveness was easy. Forgiveness was only a matter of learning how to hold on and let go at once.

'Help,' Adrian said, to no one in particular – to anyone. Anyone who was willing to hear what hadn't been said until now. Especially by his brother.

'Help,' he said, while his hands rhythmically pushed against his brother's sternum, impressing that heart to beat by its own volition.

'Help,' while neighbours ran down the driveway, and further off a fire truck blared its horn, an ambulance not far behind.

'Help,' willing his brother back from the past, bringing Noel into the present with a word neither had thought to say until now.

SIX

EPILOGUE

Seven months after the fire, Adrian walks into a supermarket, his new son asleep in his arms. He has long since put Alex and the allegations out of his mind, pushing those events to a corner he knows is there but from which he can avert his eyes, for the most part, and on most days. Today is not such a day.

While he makes his way down an aisle, a man walks past carrying a basket. He doesn't pay any attention to the man, other than to move aside a little, out of courtesy. But then he senses that the man has stopped and is looking at him and the baby. Adrian turns, sees that the man is Alex. Alex, no more than six feet away. One step towards each other and they would be within arm's reach. The closest they've been since the day Adrian was called to the office, the day of his car accident, the day the drama began. And now that he sees Alex again, he feels a familiar surge of emotion, affection, perhaps even a form of desire. But he has learned to push through that, to move forward with what is actually his. Now is the moment to take control.

They don't speak. Alex looks at the content baby boy, then

at Adrian. He nods, and Adrian nods too. Then Alex turns, and goes his own way.

★

'Adrian's back,' Glenda calls from the kitchen, as he pulls into the driveway.

She makes her way to the front door and watches Adrian unbuckle her new grandson from the car, then cradle him as he walks up the path. She holds her hands out and Adrian eases the baby from his arms into hers. She leans in and kisses the baby from forehead to nose, just as Adrian likes to do, just as she once did a long time ago with her two boys. She wasn't able to see the baby until this morning because of Vietnamese custom, some superstition or other that she didn't agree with at first, but, today being his one-month celebration, she now lets that feeling go. She is filled instead with so much love for the littlest Pomeroy, his supple skin, the smell of his newness, that she has to hold back from crying. And she can't help thinking of her own two babies, holding each of them in her arms all those years ago. It's as though her body has never forgotten the sensation of them lying there, dependent, in need of her – her milk, her warmth, her touch, her voice.

She looks up at Adrian, who gleams over his little boy, and she realises that she loves her youngest son even more now, and that she wouldn't take anything back, none of it, not even the things she didn't quite understand back then or even now, not exactly. She won't ever fully understand, she believes, and lets that feeling go as well. Just as she had to let go of Noel.

Noel. She thinks of Noel in the emergency ward, hooked up with cables, the ventilator; the way he lay there for several days without moving; the worry about brain damage; the way the family came together for him, in that moment, despite everything. Despite him. There was so much crying then – from all of them, even Mal – that now she feels as though everyone's tears somehow expelled the pressure she had once intuited would break their family. And that intuition was correct, after all, though by breaking the family it brought the family together, closer. Even Noel, in one way or another, though not consciously. Over the past seven months she has forced herself to believe that – no matter how much she continued to cry for her eldest boy, no matter how many times she wanted to crumple at the knees or not go on with routine things like making meals and washing dishes, to stop and throw her hands in the air and say out loud, *Why should I care about this when Noel is dead?* – despite those feelings, ultimately, destruction can bring about joy. And now, holding her new grandson, she knows this to be true.

Nguyet comes from the kitchen, wiping her hands on a tea towel. 'Did he sleep the whole time?' she asks Adrian, and he nods.

She sees Grace and Tam on the corduroy lounges, Grace teaching him how to play chess. She thinks about her deep love for her boys, and can't wait to show them her Vietnam. *Not long,* she thinks. *Only weeks now.*

And Adrian, of course. Her monkey. She wonders what her mother will make of him this time. Some days even Nguyet doesn't know what to make of him. She always assumed that forgiveness was something felt, not something to labour over, something to work hard at, daily, and reminds herself of the complexity of actions: that even though Adrian's showing of love for her could wane or even fail sometimes, so could her love for him. She reminds herself that love is affection, negotiation, tolerance. Even hurt. And looking at her baby boy in Glenda's arms, his sleepy face, his tiny fingers, she appreciates that all her hurt has led, in one way or another, to this happiness.

As Noo and Glenda take the shopping and his youngest into the kitchen, Adrian walks through the house to the table out the back. He sits next to Wendy, who is drinking wine and reading crime fiction. Out in the yard, Mal has the blue tarp off his kit car, which, remarkably, he managed to complete a couple of months ago. Although whenever Adrian comes over, Mal is still tinkering with something, like he is now, the driver's door open, his legs hanging out as he fiddles under the dash. His drinking hasn't stopped so his dementia has worsened, the only benefit being that grief hasn't hit him so hard – at least from what Adrian can tell.

Adrian leans over the table to pour himself a glass of grappa and looks at the picture Riley is sketching. 'Didn't know you were an artist,' he says.

Riley doesn't say that he's been drawing ideas for tattoos, or that he's drawing right now to distract himself from thinking about that day all those months ago, when his dad successfully humiliated him more than ever before, on the worst day of his life so far. Riley told himself he didn't give a shit about his dad dying, that when they got the phone call in Canberra and he heard what happened the only thought to cross his mind was that the old bastard deserved it, and he hoped going out that way was like torture because he'd tortured Riley so much over the years, even more so when he came out as trans. But then there was the funeral, and that changed how Riley felt. The change didn't come when he saw the coffin, or from listening to the speeches. It was afterwards, when Adrian came outside and sat next to him on the street kerb.

'You should know a few things about your dad,' his uncle said, 'about why he acted like he did.' Adrian went on to say that Noel had probably paid out on Riley out of fear, and that he found it difficult to accept Riley for who he is because Noel found it difficult to accept who he himself was, and that he probably felt ownership for all of Riley's decisions. Perhaps also that Noel felt Riley's choices reflected on his limitations as a father – maybe even as a person.

'That's just stupid, though,' Riley had said, scratching at the kerb with a rock.

'It sounds stupid to us, but we all have shit to deal with.'

Riley nodded. 'We all just deal with it differently,' he said.

Then Adrian had stood, looked back at the funeral home door and said, 'You can be a better person than your father was.'

Riley took that to mean that it was up to him to decide how he responded to his own problems, and part of that was how he chose to remember his father. Which is why he now wants to design his own tattoo, regardless of whether he ever gets it done. Working at the lines gives him the chance to practise some compassion for his dad. To keep thinking of him, but to shed himself of his father at the same time.

Wendy is trying to read but she's thinking of Noel in hospital, and of the funeral. She frightened herself with how much she cried that week, but she knows now that it was mostly from shock – shock brought on by the drama of what Noel had done, of how spectacularly he went out, and by the realisation that she never really knew who he was. Not to mention what he'd done to Adrian. She couldn't justify any of it.

She felt relief when he passed because she knew the crisis his actions would've brought on – that the criminal justice system he'd worked so hard for would now work him over. Sure, the police force would've offered good legal counsel and a psychiatrist, would've stuck by him for as long as they could while the media attention lasted, but in the end Noel would've come out of it all as a broken man. No, as Wendy saw it, Noel had hit the escape button, so she did too.

Moving back to Canberra was the best decision she'd made in a long time. The kids were happier, too. Though that took some time. Riley told her about getting his periods, so she sought medical advice and they began the steps towards hormone therapy. Grace hadn't coped well with her father's death or the move, but over the past few months she'd improved, settling into a new group of friends. Not to mention the boyfriend. For Wendy, living close to her mother was the most important thing: she could support her mother, and her mother could support her.

But she hadn't turned her back on the Pomeroys, and getting together today to see Noo's new little one for the first time means that the day isn't about loss but gain, which is more important. The Pomeroys, she believes, have to look forward, not backward.

Wendy watches Adrian sip his grappa. She watches him watching Riley, Mal, the sky. 'Happy?' she asks. It's a dumb sort of question, she knows, but she hopes he'll say that, yes, he is happy, for once.

But he doesn't show that he's heard her.

'Adrian?' she says, and puts her hand on his forearm. 'Hello in there ...'

It takes an extended moment before her words, her touch, bring him back. 'Sorry?' he says.

Wendy shakes her head in an amused way. 'Where did you go?' she asks.

There is a place Adrian goes to. Not a physical place, a location on a map, although it was once. *Once*. He isn't keen on that word because it happened more than once, and the word sounds a little too much like fable. Because it did happen. The materials of his memory have come apart over the years, some replaced by reproductions, and some of those reproductions have been replaced by yet more reproductions – the mind's ability to record and replay and re-record, changing memory into something which both existed and didn't exist, and yet still exists nonetheless. Without doubt.

Adrian understands these things, and has carved out a place for himself in the in-between – a place where he can sit with the six-year-old boy he once was and the twelve-year-old boy Noel once was, and the three of them can talk and tell stories to each other. The kind of stories that destroy the silences people construct around their pasts. The kind of stories that must be told, because protective silences can also be punitive.

ACKNOWLEDGEMENTS

Warm thanks go to the people who played a significant role in shaping this book: Kate Elkington, who put the fire in my belly and provided endless encouragement; Madonna Duffy, my publisher, for her commitment and unwavering enthusiasm; my astute and generous editors, Cathy Vallance, Rebecca Starford and Julian Welch; Matthew and Hoa Jennings, for endorsing my Vietnamese cultural references; and Claire, who gifted me time, space and belief.

BURNING DOWN
Venero Armanno

Charlie Smoke is living out his early retirement from the boxing ring as a bricklayer. It is the mid-1970s and his best days are behind him. He's lost his wife and daughter to his questionable past, but when he meets Holly Banks and her teenage son, Ricky, he has a chance to do things differently. As an unlikely friendship develops with Ricky, Charlie is unwittingly pulled back into the gambling underworld he thought he'd left behind. In order to make a new future, first he must help settle some old scores.

Burning Down is a searing new novel from acclaimed storyteller Venero Armanno about family, regret, love and the promise of salvation.

'Australian crime writing has never been in better hands.'
Weekend West

ISBN 978 0 7022 5970 8

HINTERLAND
Steven Lang

Tensions have been slowly building in the old farming district of Winderran. Its rich landscape has attracted a new wave of urban tree-changers and wealthy developers. But traditional loyalties and values are pushed to the brink with the announcement of a controversial dam project. Locals Eugenie and Guy are forced to choose sides, while newcomer Nick discovers there are more sinister forces at work. The personal and the political soon collide in ways that will change their fates and determine the future of the town.

In *Hinterland*, Steven Lang has created a gripping novel that captures contemporary Australia in all of its natural beauty and conflicting ambitions.

'Like Lang's other novels, *Hinterland* is rich with complex characters and ethical dilemmas that are relevant for our time. Highly recommended.'

ANZ Lit Lovers

ISBN 978 0 7022 5965 4

UQP

DANCING HOME
Paul Collis

Winner of the 2016 David Unaipon Award

Blackie and Rips are fresh out of prison when they set off on a road trip back to Wiradjuri country with their mate Carlos. Blackie is out for revenge against the cop who put him in prison on false grounds. He is also craving to reconnect with his grandmother's country.

Driven by his hunger for drugs and payback, Blackie reaches dark places of both mystery and beauty as he searches for peace. He is willing to pay for that peace with his own life.

Part road-movie, part 'Koori-noir', *Dancing Home* announces an original and darkly funny new voice.

'*Dancing Home* is at times heartbreaking, sometimes mystical, often laugh-out-loud funny, and reads like a road movie cranked up to 11. Paul Collis is a welcome and essential new voice in Australian writing.'

Readings Monthly

ISBN 978 0 7022 5975 3